Yellow-Billed Magpie

Nancy Schoellkopf

Published by Butterfly Tree Productions

Sacramento, California, USA

Publisher's note: this is a work of fiction. Names, characters, places, and incidents are either the product of the author's imagination or are used fictitiously, and any resemblance to actual persons, living or dead, business establishments, events or locales is entirely coincidental. To our knowledge, facilitated communication is no longer used in any educational facilities.

Cover design by Karen Phillips

Author photo by Gina M. Pole

ISBN-10:0692445730
ISBN-13:978-0692445730

Yellow-Billed Magpie

Butterfly Tree Publishing

For Craig

wherever you may find him

CHAPTER ONE

The morning Samantha planned to leave, a sharp-shinned hawk snatched a baby sparrow from the nest built in the corner of the back porch.

It was barely 6 AM. Samantha had only just padded into the empty kitchen on bare feet. She heard a thump and flurry outside the tall window. There followed a hissing sound—like air escaping from a leaky valve. Angelcat appeared, a black streak leaping onto the sill above the sink. Samantha darted forward, unthinking, to grab the knob and jerk the door wide. A blur of feathers. A sound like skin slapping skin. Something small and round dropped on the stoop. She looked down.

The bird was no bigger than her thumb. Wet, hairless, tiny beak open, black eyes dulled, dash of blood on its ripped throat.

Her cat was pushing against her ankles, pressing at the screen to get a look. Samantha shut the door, leaned against it. Angel yowled.

"Yes, yes, I'll get you your breakfast now."

She felt it in her solar plexus, an anxious sorrow for the sparrows, wondering if they felt anything like human grief over the loss of a child, anything like fear at being violated in their own home. The death of the baby bird also cast a pall over the anticipation of her journey, as if it were an omen of some kind. But perhaps it was time to let go of her constant search for signs, she thought as she dished up a bowl of cat food. Maybe it was time for a bit of old fashioned common sense for a change. She set the bowl on a mat near the stove. If anything the death of this baby bird reaffirmed her decision to leave. It put a period at the end of her experiment with marriage.

Angel brushed past her to eat, and she affectionately patted the cat's haunches. *What of the hawk?* she wondered. He had dropped his prize on the stoop; now he won't even get his meal. It was her fault: she shouldn't have interfered, shouldn't have opened the door. She grabbed a clean white paper towel, went outside, scooped the tiny body onto the paper. The ground was freshly watered and soft in the herb garden. She could bury it there.

Samantha had spent three years watching the birds through the seasons. When she married lawyer and county supervisor Tom Jankowsky and moved to the foothills, she had resolved to become a birder, if only junior grade. She'd bought four different field guides but was most enthralled with the common yard birds everyone else took for granted: the robins and killdeer, the scrub jays and mocking birds, the humble sparrow. It was said a sparrow perched on the crossbeam during the long hours of the crucifixion, proving its species' loyalty and ability to endure long suffering.

Tom had wanted to enclose the back of the house in glass, making a bright southern-facing sun porch for winter afternoons. But Samantha had always talked him out of it, standing with the sparrows that arrived every spring with straw and yarn to camp in the high corner of the porch until late September.

She had no trowel so she dug in the moist dirt with her fingers. She paused before covering the tiny creature, wondering at a prayer to say. She took a deep breath. "Namaste," she whispered with a quick bow of her head.

She wiped her hands on the paper towel, then tossed it in the trash can as she returned to the house. He can do it now, she thought. Tom can build his sun porch if he wants. There's no one to stop him.

As she approached the kitchen door she could see Tom staring out the window. He averted his gaze and stepped back quickly when he saw her, as if he didn't want to be caught looking for her.

Samantha hesitated, taking a deep breath. Tom had been as blatant as an open wound—and nearly as weepy too--since she'd announced her intention to leave. Samantha felt guilty. Sure, she was fudging the truth, but only to save his feelings. She did not savor the thought of yet another confrontation.

She lingered for a moment on the path, her hands tucked into the faded blue pockets of her denim jeans. She was sorry to leave these mighty pines. Paradoxically she felt taller here standing beside these giants, though of course she was still only 5'6". Maybe it was the thinner air: she had to stretch her neck to get a deep breath here. What's more, something here in this thin air made her brown eyes water, not all the time, but too often. Yeah, that's what was happening. Or maybe it was the fullness of her disappointment that forced her to stand a bit straighter, if only to contain all the new sadness stuffed between her naval and her throat.

Blinking back a few tears, Samantha felt herself circling down to a shallow spot in her psyche, a place where childhood bullies, maniacal bosses, and competitive co-workers went to dwell and fester, a dark closet so familiar she sardonically called it home base. She breathed deeply, knowing she could not allow herself to wallow in self-pity, not today when she had a long drive ahead of her. Still she could not escape the sense that she *was* her wounds: they had defined her since childhood. Now she was adding another painful gash to string with the rest, like black gems on a charm bracelet.

She was tempted to turn, as she had most other mornings, and head down the trail to a small clearing amidst oak and pine, a spot she had privately declared sacred. There she often sat on the cool ground to pray and meditate, feeling the strong pull of Divine energy coursing up and down her spine. She had taken this feeling as an affirmation that this wooded haven could be her home, that she did indeed belong here. But in recent weeks, her hands and feet began to glow during her prayer time. She knew some action was being asked of her. *I am the handmaid of the Lord:* a childhood prayer haunted her like a popular song. It was time to go back to work.

She was eager to get on the road, so she resigned herself to forego a final meditation in her favorite spot. As she looked back up at the house, it occurred to her for the first time that she was angry. Not at Tom, but at God. Hadn't she felt led here to be with this man?

With him she felt she would finally manifest the one thing that she had prayed for for so long: a child of her own. She had felt affirmed that this was the next step on her spiritual journey, but a year of failed fertility treatments had brought her here, between the house and the road, her pockets empty and her chest aching. She wondered how she could reconcile her journey now: must she surrender to what appeared to be a prescribed path or would she ever have the courage to attempt to steer her own course again?

She tugged at her chestnut hair, still damp from her shower. The sun was only pink and orange streaks in the east, yet already it promised to be a hot July day. She lifted her hair off her neck and began to braid it. Well, here was a clear marker of time's passage: in the wedding photos she had a chin length bob, now her locks dipped below her shoulders.

She entered the kitchen to find her husband stooped in front of the open refrigerator. A ruse, she thought, an attempt to look nonchalant. He eased himself to his full height and turned slowly, feigning surprise to see her up so early. "Oh, hey, Samantha," he said, his voice a shade hoarse. "Sleep okay?"

She nodded a tad too vigorously. "Yes, fine."

"That's good," he said softly. He was a handsome man, tall and lanky with curly blond hair and a square jaw. He had blue eyes and long lashes, making him almost pretty. A natural politician, in campaign photos he managed a look of exaggerated sincerity tempered with a tad of vulnerability. He wore this visage now as he stood before the refrigerator, blocking access.

Samantha shifted her weight nervously, pointing a tentative finger toward the fridge. "I'm-uh-going to cook some eggs, I think."

"Oh." He circled out of her way, never turning his back on her. She shrugged and simpered, muttered, "thanks," as she turned to grab the cardboard carton from the bottom shelf.

"You took all the books off the bookshelf near the fireplace," he said softly to her back.

She glanced back at him as she closed the refrigerator and laid the eggs on the counter near the stove. "I only took the ones that were mine," she said defensively.

"You're missing the point." His tone was deliberately even, as if struggling to maintain some control. He paused, then began again. "You kept all your books separate from mine. You did that from the beginning."

She bent down to pull a frying pan from a cupboard under the stove. "I don't know. I guess so." She shrugged, sincerely confused.

"So you never did think our marriage would work."

"What? I don't understand--"

"Everything in this house is either yours or mine; there's nothing that's ours. You planned it that way from the beginning. You always considered this a temporary arrangement, didn't you?"

"Jeez, Tom--" she began, but he interrupted.

"No, Samantha, I'm right," he interjected, his voice growing louder. "If you were honest with yourself, you'd know I was right."

She jut her chin forward and spoke in a voice that matched his in volume and vehemence. "What do you want me to say? Is that what you want me to say? Would that make you happy if I admitted that?"

He stared at her, gnawing at the corner of his mouth. He was breathing hard as if he had just run a mile, and Samantha felt bad, knowing she had surprised him with her sudden retort. Certainly he had wanted her to reassure him, to once more say something placating and conciliatory in the "it's not you, it's me" vein. But she was tired of playing softball. He cleared his throat, finally turned toward the sink to fill a glass with water. She stared at his back, praying that she wouldn't feel so uncomfortable with this silence that she might blurt out yet another apology, giving him an opening for yet another pitch to change her mind and stay. He wasn't blameless either, she reminded herself. Had he ever really loved her, or was she simply a good choice as partner, a fitting prop on his campaign brochures? She had never made such an accusation, and she was determined to make it through this final breakfast cleanly, without rancor and words of resentment. "Do you want some eggs?" she asked quietly. "I guess I'm just going to scramble some eggs." Her voice drifted off as she turned slowly to gauge his response to her olive branch.

"Look," he said, placing his water glass on the counter, "why don't I make breakfast for you while you go fill up your gas tank. You won't want to have to stop while you've got the cat in the car."

"Oh." She nodded. "Thank you, that's very thoughtful."

He responded with an exaggerated, long-suffering shrug, and she held her breath to keep from rolling her eyes. Another nice moment dashed, and that—that right there—was what had pushed her out the door. Still she got her feet to move across the tiled floor to give him a quick peck on the cheek. "I'll be right back," she said as she reached for her car keys kept on a peg by the door.

He nodded and approached the stove. "So do you really want them scrambled or would you rather have them poached?"

She graced him with a small smile. "Yeah, poached would be good."

She put her hand on the doorknob. "See," he replied. "I do know what you like."

She bit her lip and went out the door without another word.

***

This will be the last drive, Samantha thought later, as she traversed the twisting road between the foothills and the valley. A rousing Celtic reel played softly on the public radio station, but soon Samantha knew she would reach a spot where her radio would cut out and she would travel twelve or fifteen miles—thirty to forty minutes—in silence, with nothing but her own thoughts for company. It was a thickly wooded area where the road sunk low, and that fern-like creeper, Mountain Misery, grew wild, suffusing her nostrils with its acrid perfume.

She never substituted a CD for the loss of the radio signal, but in her frequent commutes while she and Tom were dating, Samantha anticipated this spot as a kind of retreat or prayer break, a small space in the middle between two busy lives where she could assess her emotional temper and her spiritual health.

This day as the road dipped into shadow and quiet descended, she thought of previous sojourns, usually solo, without even her cat for reflection. Some days she had chanted aloud long neglected mantras and Catholic hymns. But she had to admit to herself she'd spent an inordinate amount of time thinking about men. Three men in particular played on her mind. She wondered if there would ever be another man who would capture her devotion as these three had. She wondered if she cared.

During the early trips she would think of Tom and the wedding, allowing herself to surrender to a bit of girlish glee at the prospect of the upcoming fairy tale spectacle. She'd think how Tom had talked her into a formal sit-down dinner with prime rib and new potatoes. She'd think about the chocolate cake with raspberry filling she'd picked out despite Tom's objections. Then she'd stray into dangerous territory and think about the dress. Tom had deferred to her insistence that it was bad luck for the groom to see the bride's gown before the wedding. In reality she couldn't have cared less about this superstition. She simply wanted to make her choice without his badgering input. But his elderly mother had butt in to advocate for some Victorian design with a high waist and high neckline. She had managed to dodge that bullet, diplomatically pleading that it would be much too warm, even in September, for such heavy fabric, and Mrs. Jankowsky hadn't said another word. Samantha chose instead a pale peach raw silk and lace tea length sheath, sleeveless with a scalloped V-neck. She was 38 years old, for crying out loud, she wasn't going to do herself up like Miss Havisham in an ornate outfit that could easily do double duty for a girl at a quinciñera or junior prom. She wanted to look dignified, though she did surrender to the suggestion of a spray of orchids in her hair.

Still whenever she entered a bridal shop or looked at the bridal magazines her soon to be mother-in-law thrust at her, her mind would stray to that Valentine's Day years ago when she bought the big flouncy white wedding gown at the thrift store with Charlie. That dress had it all: a fitted bodice, long lacy sleeves and a seven-foot train. Every inch of the neckline, cuffs and train was covered in elaborate beadwork: fat pearls arranged in clusters of grapes and butterflies. It was magnificent. Charlie had zipped her into it, then stepped back, nearly gasping behind her as she twirled in front of the mirror. The sales clerk, young and blonde, her hair in braids, ambled by to take a look too. "I have the perfect shoes to go with that," she gushed. Charlie had objected politely, saying shoes would not be necessary, because "we're not quite ready to make a purchase tonight." Samantha had turned to give him a wicked grin. "Oh, I'm buying this dress, baby," she told him. His head bobbed back in surprise and he lifted his hands as if confronted by the law. "Hey, whatever you want, O'Malley." The sales clerk ran off to the far corner to retrieve "the dreamiest" shoes.

"No worries," Samantha assured him. "I have no intention of dragging you to Reno tonight."

"Or any night," he muttered. She gave him a narrow-eyed glare, and he quickly amended his snide remark. "Well, at least not anytime soon."

She rolled her eyes and turned again to the mirror to admire her overly adorned reflection. Samantha had spent a decade and a half dating intellectuals and nerds, computer geeks and professorial types. Charlie was all this and more: he was fun, funny, smart--and okay, the very first time she met him he had taken her breath away. Every time they made love her heart broke open like the crust on a loaf of bread that splits in the warmth of the oven. She was undeniably smitten, perhaps even in love for the first time at the age of 29. But he was untamed, erratic, unreliable. She told herself it was an opportunity to practice living in and cherishing each moment. So on this night, she would not allow his ambivalence to ruin her good mood. "It's just a fun dress," she declared with a bit of forced bravado. "Why wouldn't I buy it?"

"You'll probably use it someday," he offered without commitment, and this remark annoyed her more than the last, maybe because he didn't seem to know that this gooey confection of a dress was not her style at all.

She swung around quickly and took a step toward him, seductively pushing her breasts against his chest and lifting her face to his. "Of course I'm going to use it, but not someday—today! Let's go dancing! I'll bet no matter where we go they'll give us free drinks!"

He laughed at her brazenness, but that was in fact what they did. She purchased the dress—a $14.95 Valentine's Day special, along with the $2 oyster colored slingback pumps the sales clerk picked out for her, and off they went to the Doubletree Inn off Exposition Boulevard. She clattered across the asphalt parking lot in the flimsy shoes, while Charlie trudged behind her, the train of her new dress balled up in his arms like a live turkey. They danced to the oldies and when they sat down the bartender sent them two free champagne cocktails. "Too sweet," she told Charlie.

"No," he said in a sexy growl. "You're too sweet." Then they went back to her house and made love. He pleaded with her to keep the dress on as he began to expertly peel back layer after layer of tulle and lace, searching for the simple and familiar cotton panties she always wore, but she objected since there were stays on the sides, so he flipped her over to slowly toy with satin-covered buttons, and—

That would be when she would take a deep breath and shut down this playful and cherished memory. But instead of guiding her thoughts back to Tom and their upcoming nuptials, her mind would inevitably wander to Craig. She had met him her first year of teaching when she had a bully for a principal, two whiners for assistants, and she wondered every Monday if this would be the week she would quit her job for good. Craig was a substitute custodian assigned long term to the night shift. He had propped her up and held her hand, and she'd made it through. "You are special," he told her. "Don't you understand that I've come here to tell you this? Vacuuming the room, dusting the chalk trays—that's my avocation! My true purpose in being here is to talk to you, to deliver this message: you are important."

She wondered sometimes what Craig would think of her marriage to Tom. Was she doing the right thing when she quit teaching special education students to take on the role of full time hostess to renowned lawyer and county supervisor Tom Jankowsky? Sure, Tom was a big fish in a little pond, Samantha had been aware of that. Yet she had been more naïve than she had realized. She knew that now. *You don't know what you don't know,* she told herself, downshifting as the road dipped.

Three men, she thought again. And I was stupid enough to

marry the only one I didn't love.

CHAPTER TWO

She felt an itch and turned to run her long tongue down her muscular back. Her fur was thick and covered with brown and yellow spots. "Ah, I am a jaguar this time," she thought to herself. She lifted a massive paw to her mouth, how satisfying, the sensation of sandpaper rough tongue between her furry toes.

She looked up. The air was thick with moisture. Deep purple blossoms yawned on rubbery vines near her neck and ears, green leathery ferns bobbed around her shoulders. She looked down. She was high in the air, gazing at tangled limbs and vines, green and fluorescent pinks, neon blues and yellows. Everything seemed to be swaying with misty rain and the movement of tiny creatures: ants, spiders, rodents. Dramatic red wings of a macaw swept past; her massive neck darted to follow its flight with her gaze. She bolted onto her haunches, tempted to leap at the bird, barely able to resist the powerful force of adrenaline in her throat. She swallowed, pressing her cat ears hard against her head. She settled back onto the limb, her heart pounding in her chest. A monkey swung from a branch below her, and she salivated. She was hungry, so hungry.

A flurry of wings at her ear distracted her. She turned to see a yellow-billed magpie hovering near her face. Involuntarily she swiped at it with her right paw, but the bird flitted out of reach. And then she was falling off the limb, falling through a wet blur of green and yellow and fuchsia.

Samantha bolted awake, breathing hard in the dim light. Five AM: a half hour before the alarm was set to go off. She rolled onto her back and stared at soft gray shadows locked onto the ceiling.

New house, new job, but same old bed. She'd slept in this antique sleigh bed for eighteen years before her marriage. When she moved in with Tom in the foothills they'd put this bed in the guest room. It was smaller than a queen, a full to be exact, somewhat utilitarian, but even more comfortable than before since Tom had insisted on buying a new mattress and box spring when it arrived at his house. He'd always been polite when he slept over at her midtown bungalow, but when her furniture became community property he decided it needed an upgrade.

Samantha thought it was big of him to let her take the mattress with her when she left, but she decided not to mention it. She'd learned over the years to mention neither debts not slights: it was just easier that way. Best to move on, apply salve to your wounded psyche in private, and get on with it. This constant talking talking talking seemed to solve nothing.

Angelcat snored softly on the right side of the bed closest to the wall. That had been Angel's favorite spot before the marriage, and she'd taken it up quickly again now that they lived alone—"just us girls." She whispered the phrase aloud as she reached to pat Angel's head. The cat's eyes slit open and she stretched with typical feline grace. "Just us girls," Samantha repeated a little louder, knowing the phrase that she said frequently now to the cat, was fraught with pride at her own independence and resilience, but also with sadness. She wondered again as she anticipated the day ahead if she had made a mistake coming back to Sacramento. She had been raised here, had always considered it home, but what did that mean really? Her brother had long been settled in the midwest, teaching mathematics at Northwestern outside Chicago. Her mother was dead more than a decade from breast cancer. Her father had died suddenly of a heart attack shortly before Samantha started dating Tom. She didn't need a psychoanalyst to tell her that her hasty marriage was an attempt to build herself a new family. So what if it was? But maybe she needed a shrink to explain this silly decision to sink back into this hot valley and return to the classroom.

Samantha had left a fifteen-year career teaching special education when she married Tom and moved to the foothills. She had loved working with the children, though school district politics often proved too melodramatic for her liking. With working conditions like these, Samantha had needed little persuasion to leave this quagmire and start a new phase in her life. Tom had been eager to give her children of her own. But that goal had proved unattainable and Samantha was unsure how to discern a new direction. Was it really the best choice to return to her old job in her old hometown?

If she'd been craving the familiar maybe she should have returned to her former employer, the sprawling school district that served three quarters of the city's families. No, she was satisfied she'd been smart to accept a position in a small but growing district on the north side of town. But maybe she should have returned to the old midtown neighborhood where she had set down roots twenty-two years ago when she was in college. Instead she had bought a town house in a new subdivision near her new school.

As usual she had let her intuition guide her. When she job-hunted online the Northgate District had more openings than anywhere else. It seemed natural to apply there. When she drove to their sparkling new district office, she'd seen dozens of signs directing traffic to the model homes at the new subdivision. This kind of place had never been her style, but that day it called to her. She liked the energy here, so close to the confluence of the Sacramento and American Rivers. She'd jumped in with both feet.

Still she doubted herself. None of it felt comfortable yet. Although it had been less than a month, she worried it never would be. Maybe this strange series of dreams in which she starred as one animal after another was trying to alert her to a desire for something far more exotic.

She sat up and clicked on a lamp. Something that was familiar was the frantic pace of the classroom, the joyful but demanding nature of children. The work was satisfying but exhausting. Was she really up for it again?

The radio alarm snapped on. Her feet hit the floor. Time to get to school.

***

Ten-year-old Echo Abernathy pushed the new yellow pencil across the table with a quick flick of her right fingers. "No," she sneered in a bold but modulated voice. "I don't want to do your stupid math paper."

On the other side of the table, Samantha composed her face into a practiced affect of nonchalance as she lifted the rejected pencil. "Oh, okay," she said with a shrug. She turned to deliver a high five to the round-faced boy sitting next to Echo. "Aidan is doing a great job. Thank you, Aidan." Aidan beamed. His blue almond shaped eyes, the unmistakable mark of his Down Syndrome, narrowed even as his cheeks puffed out with pride.

Then the teacher turned to the dark-haired girl at her right hand. "And Luisa! You are amazing!" The girl rocked rapidly in her chair at the mention of her name, abruptly lifting her flat left palm and bouncing it repeatedly against her full lips. "C'mon, Lulu. It's okay," Samantha soothed the autistic child. She held Luisa's palm aloft so she could give the girl a gentle encouraging pat. "Good job, Lulu."

Echo crumpled the offending sheet of addition problems. "Lulu never has to do anything!" she complained. "You're just happy if she doesn't drool."

Samantha sucked in a quick breath, momentarily stunned by the bitter comment. Echo threw the wadded paper at her teacher. "I won't do it," she announced again, and still Samantha felt calm despite this defiance. Then Echo did something else. This ten-year-old girl, this four foot tall dynamo, small for her age, really, this wind-swept wonder with long honey colored hair pulled back with a pink scrunchy, her ponytail slightly askew since lunch time—Samantha had noticed this, of course, had wondered if there had been an altercation or race or fall that might have accounted for the less than fastidious do--Echo pushed back her chair, pushed back her bangs, wiped her quivering lips with the back of her fist, fastened a reptilian glare at Samantha and said, "You Can't Make Me."

Samantha leapt onto the table (or perhaps she only imagined that she did so), her tooled leather cowboy boots clicking on the faux pine, sticky with Elmer's glue and teacher's sweat and children's spit and she stamped her feet and swung a knotted jump rope and cried out, "So I can't make ya, huh? I can't make ya? Well kid, tell me something I don't know! Go on! Tell me! Who do you think you're dealing with here? You think I was born yesterday? You think I just fell off the turnip truck? I know better than anybody: I can't make you do nothing! I never get what I want! I am completely powerless!

14

I know that! And you think you're so smart!"

Samantha squeezed Lulu's hand and was back in her body, sitting silently staring at tiny Echo who stood like an angry animal, using instinctive tricks to make herself look bigger—pointy elbows akimbo, shoulders approaching her ears, nostrils flared, eyes dilated. Samantha rose, pulling Lulu with her. "I hope you'll make a better choice, Echo," she said in a near whisper, as she led Lulu from the table. "C'mon, Aidan," she said to the boy, cocking her head. Aidan followed.

Samantha led Lulu and Aidan to a table of children staffed by her aide Rose on the other side of the room. Rose stood to take Lulu's hand from Samantha, a practiced routine. "Aidan, you go to Valerie's table," Samantha directed, indicating a space in the back of the room.

"You can still make a good choice, Echo," Samantha repeated in a singsong voice. She paused at her desk in the corner and pulled from the bottom drawer a silk lei, a garish necklace of orange and pink petals to fling around her neck. "Yes, I hope you make a good choice and do some work, because the rest of us are going to Hawaii. When we finish our math we are heading for the catamarans and setting off for Kauai and Maui and Oahu and everybody who does their work will get chocolate covered macadamia nuts!—so make a good choice, Echo!"

But Echo was tugging at her scrunchy, grabbing fistfuls of her own hair, and gritting her teeth. "You are a mean teacher," she screeched, "and a bad woman!" Samantha looked at her nonplussed. Mean teacher she was willing to concede, but despite her failed marriage, she thought she'd done a pretty good job of being a woman. Before she had a chance to respond, Echo pushed over a chair and ran out of the room.

Samantha didn't know whether to burst out laughing or crying. She imagined herself picking up a bullhorn, shouting, "Cut! That's a wrap!" as if the class was an elaborate reality show and they had all conspired to, and had succeeded in, capturing something real juicy. Still staring at the doorway through which Echo had made her exit, Samantha finally shrugged. At least this powerlessness felt familiar.

"I need to write a behavior plan for that child," she said, glancing first at one aide, then at the other.

"She's a tough one," agreed junior aide Valerie, new and eager to please. She rose from her seat, her long fingers spread and resting lightly on the table in front of her. The younger aide was in her mid-20s and filled with energy. Nearly six-feet tall, a long black braid trailing down her back, she looked the part of the loyal soldier awaiting orders. "Do you want me to go after her?" she asked.

"Echo doesn't belong here," senior aide Rose said decisively. She gave her large gray head a steady shake. She was short with broad shoulders and a double chin. Her movements were often slow and deliberate, but she was not to be underestimated. The woman was fierce as a bulldog. "Have you put in a change of placement request yet?" she asked in her deep, no-nonsense voice.

Now was not the time for such discussions so Samantha ignored all questions. "I'll be right back," she said. "But if I'm not. . ." She switched to a stage whisper. "The candy's in here." She cocked a thumb at the top drawer of the file cabinet, then resumed a booming voice of encouragement. "Keep working, my hula babies!"

She darted out the door, then paused to get her bearings. It was only her third week at Rosa Parks' Elementary School, and Echo was giving her no honeymoon. But it felt oh so familiar: could she take comfort in that? she wondered wryly. Still stinging from her divorce, the veteran of countless confrontations with special education students in a 15-year career, Samantha was no stranger to combat. Nor to failure. She took a deep breath and strode across the quad.

She found Echo in the cafeteria, pounding her tiny fists on the counselor's office door in the back of the room. "Mrs.West isn't here today, Echo," she said. Echo tipped back her head, closed her eyes, and let loose with a high-pitched theatrical scream. The heads of the custodian (who was mopping the floor) and of the lunch lady (who was counting her receipts) both bobbed in perfect unison to give Samantha identical looks of stunned annoyance. Samantha winced. "Sorry," she mouthed silently. Custodian and lunch lady both turned away, but Samantha couldn't help but note their eye rolls and headshakes. Yet again: the familiarity of judgment. Feels like home.

Samantha offered a hand to Echo. "Let's go someplace safe," she said, infusing her voice with as much soothing patience as she could muster.

Echo reared back, drawing her hands to her chest. "I don't want to go to the office!"

"We need to go to a safe place so you can calm down."

"I don't want to go to the office."

"I'll send Valerie in to sit with you. You won't be alone."

"I don't want my Mom to come and find me in the office." The girl's voice sounded panicky. Samantha felt a swell of sympathy in her throat and chest. Echo had been released from the foster system back into her mother's care for less than six months: pleasing Mom right now was a high priority. "You can come back to the room before Mom comes to pick you up," Samantha promised. "That's not a problem." She thrust her hand out again. "C'mon now," she said insistently.

"You won't tell my Mom I got in trouble?"

Samantha sighed, unwilling to negotiate further. "I want to tell Mom you made a good choice and went to a safe place."

Echo looked down for a moment then slowly took Samantha's hand. She allowed the teacher to lead her away.

Samantha passed Principal Convivio in the hallway after dropping Echo off by the secretary's desk. "I'm leaving Echo, but my aide will be in to watch her," Samantha told him.

Jon Convivio, sixty-four years old, was mere months away from retirement. He had a full head of curly white hair, an angular jaw and high cheekbones. He lifted his bushy eyebrows. "Love the necklace," he said slyly. "So what time do they start serving mai tais on the Lido deck?"

She fingered her lei a bit self-consciously, yet she leapt right in. "When I find out," she deadpanned, "you'll be the first to know."

CHAPTER THREE

At the end of the day, Samantha took Lulu's hand and strolled out to the traffic circle that constituted the school bus stop just around the corner from her classroom. Lulu was a beautiful child with skin as flawless as coral rose petals. Tall for her age, yet willowy, often perched on her tiptoes, her long fingers curled upward, she seemed as thin and flighty as an autumn leaf. Were it not for her heavy crown of ropy brown curls, she might blow away in a breeze.

Samantha saw that Mrs. Schwartz, her next door neighbor, the special ed teacher with whom she shared a wall, was standing outside her own classroom door, yelling something Samantha could not make out as a few girls darted across the parking lot.

Bunny Schwartz was 50ish, tall and wiry, with tight leathery skin and a cap of white blonde hair that hugged her head. She invariably wore a pair of tooled leather cowboy boots, whether with skirts or jeans, even with what seemed to be her favorite outfit—a polyester tracksuit. Samantha had to concede the older woman always looked comfy.

"This parking lot is an accident waiting to happen," Bunny complained in her husky voice, hoarse from yelling. "I swear I'm going to teach these kids to use the crosswalk if it's the last thing I do!"

She turned to shake her head woefully at Samantha, then grinned. "I'm an expert at breaking wild ponies," she bragged. "They just don't know it yet."

Samantha nodded with a forced smile. As the newbie on staff, she was still playing it cautious, trying to keep an open mind, but she'd never felt the ability to bully children into compliance was something worth boasting about. "Those girls don't know they've met their match, I guess," Samantha said with mock perkiness as she strode past.

Bunny nodded enthusiastically. "No, they do not!" she called after her.

Samantha quickened her pace, but even after she'd settled Lulu onto the bus and thanked the driver, she found Bunny still standing on the lawn waiting for her. "How's it going?" Bunny drawled easily. "Are you settling in all right? I've been so busy with my own class, quite a bunch this year, but yeah, I've been thinking of you, and wondering how you're settling in, because I'm right next door, so if you need anything you just let me know."

"Thanks," Samantha said, making an effort to be friendly. "I appreciate that."

Bunny stepped closer. "No problem because you know, I've been in this district for well over a decade, and believe you me, I know where the bodies are buried."

Bunny winked and Samantha nodded nervously, trying to think of some pertinent closing comment. A man's voice disturbed her reverie. "I don't believe it," he shouted, and Samantha felt the hair rise on the back of her neck. She turned toward the sound. "Ms Omm! Is that really you, girl? I can't believe it! Let me take a look at you!"

A dark haired man with golden eyes was striding toward her. Charlie Easter! Samantha felt her throat fall into her chest. He was as lean as ever with the same urgent gait of the high school sprinter he used to be. His temples were graying but he still had the ironic upside down smile and crinkled eyes that had always charmed her.

She hadn't seen him in at least five years, but she'd thought of him often enough. During the marriage to Tom, when Samantha had been busy supervising the caterers as they set up for one of Tom's parties of clients, associates, and acquaintances, she'd look at the matching table cloths and napkins and slip covers and she'd involuntarily wonder, what would Charlie think of all this? Or later, when the gathering was in full swing, and she was dressed to the nines in a silk skirt and lace blouse, but feeling alienated by small talk and small town cliquishness, then the memory of Charlie's eyes or hands would come to her unbidden, and she'd feel weak in the knees with a desire for another time and place. She'd think of him too when she sat alone in the mornings on the porch watching the phoebes and titmice and scrub jays in the fruit trees. She'd think of him when she was eating a damn hamburger for crying out loud. But the specter of him was so much simpler, more predictable, less dramatic than the actual article, that to see him coming toward her like this tempted her to turn tail and run, right into the parking lot where she could jump into her car and just keep driving. But where? She had no sanctuary, no place to go, so she sunk her full weight down into her practical crepe-soled shoes and waited, wrapping her arms tight around her waist to keep her heart from jumping out of her mouth.

"Mister-E," she greeted him gamely, slurring his name so it sounded like "mystery," and Mr. E clapped his hands and nearly doubled over with laughter. He bolted upright again and took those few final steps toward her, his arms extended as if to embrace her, but she kept one hand protectively across her chest, thrusting the other forward to shake his. He stopped to give her a scolding look at her formality, but grabbed her hand nonetheless. "I can't believe it's you, O'Malley. It's so good to see you, Ms Omm."

Samantha felt herself blushing, feeling Bunny's gaze burning upon her. "Do you know Charlie?" she asked the other teacher.

"No, we passed in the staff room this morning, but we didn't get a chance for an introduction."

Charlie reluctantly released Samantha's hand to turn and grasp Bunny's. "Charlie Easter," he told her. "Subbing for the PE teacher this week. Ms Omm and I used to work together in the City District."

"Ms Omm?" Bunny asked.

Samantha shook her head embarrassed. "It stands for O'Malley. And because I like to meditate. Charlie's clever that way, so be forewarned."

Bunny nodded, suddenly speechless. "Okay."

"And you better be careful of Samantha too," Charlie noted.

"She's the one who came up with Mystery."

"Oh, I did not. You named yourself that. I'm just the only one who realized how well it fit and consented to call you that."

"Mystery, huh?" Bunny interjected.

"Mister Easter," Samantha explained. "Mr. E—but if you blend it together--

"Oh, I see," Bunny said, "Mystery."

"Because I'm a mystery." He stared unabashed at Samantha, and despite her better judgment she couldn't help but smile back at him too.

"Do you want to see my classroom?" she asked him, tempted by yet another familiar feeling his appearance had sparked in her.

"Yeah, show me your classroom," he agreed.

"You can get there quicker through here," Bunny offered sweeping her arm toward her own door.

"That's okay," Samantha said, wishing Bunny would go away. "I want him to see the entryway; I've got something special over there."

"Oh, really?" Bunny's interest was piqued. "I'd like to see that too."

"She's lying so we can be alone," Charlie jumped in.

"Charlie!" Samantha protested. "That's not true."

"You don't mind, do you?" he said softly, managing to inject his words with a teasing charm Samantha knew so well. He gently squeezed Bunny's arm. "We have some catching up to do."

Bunny laughed, but Samantha felt mortified. "I don't mind. I've got a lot of catching up to do myself—on paperwork." Still laughing she ducked into her own classroom, and shut the door.

"Jeez, Charlie," Samantha said, half-whine, half-scold, as she took off toward her own classroom door. He bolted after her, catching her as she rounded the corner. He grabbed her shoulders and spun her around. "What?" she said, trying to stifle a smile.

He carefully reached down and gently lifted her left hand. "I see no ring," he observed.

She took a deep breath. "You see correctly," she conceded. "No ring."

He stepped back to bow, bending over to touch his lips to her fingers with a continental flourish. Rising to gaze at her face, he grinned. "Dinner, Ms Omm?"

She smiled and narrowed her eyes. "You buying, Mystery?"

***

He arrived at her house with a grocery sack from Bel Air. "You'll miss the Natural Food Co-op out here," he warned her as she opened the door. She gestured downward to point out the chocolate brown and blue Mexican tile in the entryway. Certainly this would impress him. It was the kind of thing he used to like. But he was chattering on, pulling lemons, fresh herbs and mushrooms from his paper bag. Samantha was elated, struck with the realization that he was trying to impress her too. "Chardonnay," he announced, displaying a bottle. "Is that still your favorite?"

"Oh, I think it will suffice," she said. She couldn't stop smiling and she hated herself for it.

"Where's the kitchen?" he asked. She pointed to the left. He looked away from her face, seemingly aware of his surroundings for the first time. "Is that an atrium?" he asked.

She nodded. "Every room looks out on it."

"Okay," he said. "Now I get it. An atrium in the center of your house—almost worth moving to the burbs for."

"I'm not in the burbs," she said emphatically. "This is still the city." She continued to point him toward the kitchen.

"Oh, c'mon," he said as he set his bag on the counter. "This may be within city limits, but it's got all the marks of suburbia. They're plowing under the rice fields to build tract housing and strip malls."

"It's a nice house in a nice neighborhood near my workplace—and I can afford it. Stop harassing me."

He stopped talking as he pulled something rolled in white paper from his bag. "I'm sorry," he said softly. "Guess you've had an interesting couple of years."

"Interesting," she agreed, suddenly nervous under his gaze. She had come home from school while he shopped, and she had deliberately chosen frumpy clothes to entertain him in: loose pants with an elastic waist, an oversized T-shirt. Now she felt warm. She licked her lips. "Yeah," she affirmed. "It was interesting." She turned away to get out a corkscrew and he took it from her hand.

"I'll do that," he said. "You get me a frying pan and a large saucepan to cook some rice."

They stopped talking as they set to their appointed tasks. "Wine glasses," he mused, his eyes scanning the closed kitchen cupboards. "Hmmm, I'm guessing here!" He opened the correct door to find her mother's crystal. "How well I know you, O'Malley," he bragged.

She shrugged, determined to feign aloofness, but secretly spooked whenever he did something like that. He handed her a glass and she took a sip. "Nice."

"This is better than nice," he countered. "Because I'm drinking it with you."

"Oh, no!" she cried with a grin. "Don't you try that charm crap on me, Mystery. I'll have none of that. I know you too well!"

"You probably know me better than anybody, O'Malley. You're the only one I can't fool, Sam."

She lifted her glass. "And maybe that's as good as it gets," she said a touch of sadness in her voice.

He clicked his glass against hers. "To better times," he said. "Things can always get better." He sipped his wine. "Things can always get worse too, but we're not going to go there. Not tonight."

He leaned closer and she backed away. "I'm getting pretty hungry, Charlie. You planning on cooking this stuff or shall I call a pizza parlor?"

"A pizza parlor?" he shouted dramatically. "You cut me to quick, woman. Let me at the stove. I'll fix you up a feast!"

He cooked steamed sea bass in a lime and coconut milk sauce that they ate over rice, with a spinach and mushroom salad on the side. "Where'd you get this bread?" she asked as she sopped a crusty chunk in the last of the milky sauce.

"Panera."

"Oh." She was disappointed she had moved to a neighborhood of chain stores and restaurants, but it couldn't be helped.

"So what are you going to do with this atrium?" he asked, standing to gaze out the window.

"It gets lots of sun out there," Samantha noted as she gnawed on her bread. "I'd love to have a tropical forest here—with hibiscus and ferns and bougainvillea and, uh. . ." Her voice trailed off as she stared out the window into the currently bare space. Suddenly a tall Mexican pyramid rose out of the dirt in her atrium, and she blinked in surprise at the vision.

"You'd be smarter to put in drought tolerant plants, Sam," he said, sipping his wine. "Yarrow, rock roses, and oh, Matilija Poppies. Have you ever seen those? Big beautiful blossoms, white petals with a yellow center. They look like sunnyside-up eggs! You'd like them."

She gave him a noncommittal shrug. "Maybe."

"Well," he continued, "we don't exactly have the climate for a tropical paradise here anymore."

"Hey," she replied with a feisty edge to her voice, "there'll be plenty of water if Charlie Easter keeps raining on my parade!" She laughed then stood abruptly to clear the table. Angel appeared out of nowhere to trot after her into the kitchen.

"You know," Charlie said, as he gathered dishes to follow her, "they've started metering the water here. Did you know that?"

"They have not!" she exclaimed as she stacked dishes by the

sink. "Have they?'

"It's true." He raised his hands near his chest defensively. "I'm not lying."

"Why would they do that?" she asked rhetorically.

"Why didn't they do that decades ago?"

"Hey, I live in a valley between two rivers! It's our water!"

"You Californians and your excess! Just open up the taps and let the water run out." Again he laughed, affecting a tone of mock melodrama. "Have you no shame?"

She shook her head as she placed a bowl in the dishwasher. "You're after the wrong culprit. I've never even had a dishwasher before."

"Not even in the foothills?"

"No, we had this old rambling ranch house up there. Built in the 20s. Tom was slowly updating it. I told him don't bother with the kitchen. I'm used to an old gas stove and a sink full of dishes. What do I need modern appliances for?"

"Nice for entertaining maybe," he said in a suggestive tone.

She gave him a coy smile. He was fishing, trying to find out what her life had been like with Tom. She shrugged. "He usually hired a caterer for such things," she said with exaggerated nonchalance.

He roared with laughter as he refilled the wine glasses. "Good for keeping up appearances, I suppose."

She sipped her wine and led him to the living room. The furnishings were a mixture of old and new: new couch, new wing chairs and side tables. But there were many items Charlie might recognize: her Georgia O'Keefe prints, her mother's Hummel's, her grandmother's Mission style rocking chair, and of course her old green and blue Persian rug that she's bought in an antique store nearly two decades ago. She and Charlie had rolled around on that plush woolen fabric more than once.

She sunk into her regular spot on the brown leather couch, and he sat beside her. She took a deep breath, suddenly aware of the soft shadow his evening beard was casting on his ruddy jaw, the dark hairs on the back of his wrists and forearms. She wondered if it'd be better for her to move to one of the new chairs on the other side of the coffee table. But instead she took another sip of wine, willing to risk the temptation that came with his nearness.

"So," Charlie continued, "I imagine you had to keep up a pretty active social schedule, considering your husband's position."

Samantha fingered the stem of her wine glass, finally looking up. "Look, Tom is a nice man," she said. "I don't want to complain or gossip about him. He works hard in his law practice; he always has. We had a very comfortable life together."

"And yet you're back in the valley," he said with a slight question in his voice.

"So I am." She leaned back, and stared at him, hoping to convey that the subject was closed.

He leaned back too, message received. "Okay, I'm sorry," he said. "So tell me, what did you do up there? Did you teach?"

"No, I was a lady of leisure. It was very pleasant. I volunteered at the library. I did little story corners twice a week for kids. That was fun. I took classes in knitting and quilting. I learned to make peach jam—we had both a peach and a nectarine tree on our property. It was great."

"So you didn't just move to the foothills," Charlie teased. "You moved to the 50s."

She rolled her eyes at him. "Smart ass," she mumbled. She put her wine glass on a coaster on one of the new end tables, then stretched and yawned. "Gee, Charlie, it was like a restful sabbatical for me. It was nice, okay?"

"Okay." He lifted her foot, began to knead her instep.

She closed her eyes and breathed deeply, trying to ignore a haunting concern. This felt so good, so familiar, and yet—

She opened her eyes and pulled herself upright. "So how's your son? How's Dale?" she asked.

Charlie sat up a bit straighter too, resting her foot in his lap. "He's good. Geneva moved to Carmichael, so Dale's going to Rio Americano now. He's seventeen--"

"Seventeen! Really?"

"Yeah, he's a senior. He was on the varsity basketball team last year. Second string but he got minutes nearly every game. He's applying to colleges-- Davis, Santa Cruz. Not sure what he wants to major in, but that's okay."

"What about your alma mater, Charlie? Is he considering Dartmouth at all?"

"God, no!" he exclaimed. "I don't want him to go that route. The ivy league curse stops with me!"

She laughed, knowing well that she had struck a nerve. "Such a whiner, Mystery!"

"Sam, you have no idea how much that kind of academic competition can scar a kid. You had nothing comparable in your peaceful little Sacramento valley upbringing."

She tapped her chin with an index finger, affecting a Betty Boop-like demeanor. "Oh, we women know nothing of competition. We have no idea what's it's like to not fit in, to not measure up."

He sighed. "Jeez, you've got me apologizing left and right tonight, Sam. Were you always this tough on me?"

She touched his arm and gave him a sympathetic half smile. "I've always been that tough on myself. I think we have that in common."

He nodded and squeezed her foot. They sat in silence for a long moment, Charlie staring into space, Samantha staring at him. *Any second now,* she thought, *he may swing my feet off his lap, stand up and go home.* She swallowed hard, wondering if maybe she would like to share a few things about her marriage with him, if maybe she would unveil a few wounds she had planned to keep secret. Was this the right moment, was Charlie the right person? She looked down at her hands. Did she have an ulterior motive? Revelations sometimes bring sudden intimacy: is that what she was angling for? Or did she just want to give utterance to this pain, to share it with someone other than Tom? She drew a sharp breath and Charlie turned to look at her. She leaned toward him. "I found out I can't have children," she said softly.

He said nothing for a moment, still holding her foot, gauging her emotions.

"You know," she said with a reluctant shrug, "that's kind of why I married Tom. Last chance for a baby!"

"Sam," he scoffed. "What do you mean, last chance? You're— what? Still in your 30s, right?"

"I'm 42."

"That's not so old, you have plenty of time--"

That's when the damn broke. "Aren't you listening?" she blurted, her voice cracking. "I said I can't! It's not possible."

He leaned toward her, firmly grasping her ankles. "Okay, slow down," he soothed. "Tell me what happened."

She lifted her wine glass, took a rapid gulp. "We tried for a year. Finally we both went to a doctor—a specialist of course; Tom wouldn't have wanted it any other way. So the doc said it had something to do with the PH balance in my womb—a hostile uterus or some such thing." She met Charlie's uncomfortable smile with one of her own. "It's okay," she said, waving her hand, "you can laugh. Anyway, we tried fertility shots and artificial insemination—with my husband's sperm, of course. I wouldn't have wanted to do it with anyone else's sperm, you know."

Charlie bowed his head. "You've got to stop giving me such great set up lines when I'm sensing that this isn't a good time to joke."

She pulled her foot away from him, thinking this hadn't been such a good idea. She lifted her shoulders toward her ears, and she planted her feet on the floor. "It's okay, you get the idea. I don't need to bore you with details."

He leaned forward and put his arm around her shoulders. "I'm sorry; I want to know—if you want to tell me. It's up to you, but don't let my clumsy jokes stop you, okay?"

She breathed deeply again. There was something so comfortable about Charlie, and she realized this was why she wanted to tell him. He had always been a good listener. A rare thing in a man, rarer in a lover. She leaned into his shoulder.

"It's a pretty short story really," Samantha told him. "After a year and a half of painful tests and treatments, they proposed in vitro fertilization. You know, they'd take some of my eggs and some of his sperm and mix them together in a Petri dish and then implant them in my uterus. It's not a pretty process, rather invasive actually. For the woman, that is. Harvesting those eggs is not a pleasant way to go. For the man, it's no big deal, he just masturbates in a cup." She paused, but Charlie neither snickered nor spoke. "Anyway," she continued. "I decided I couldn't do it." Again she paused. "I just couldn't go on a journey like that with someone I didn't love."

He tightened his grip on her shoulders. "I'm sorry," he said.

"I know."

They sat silently for a minute. "But Sam," he said, "you may not be completely unable--"

"Charlie, no," she said. "The doctor said no. I can't have children. Not ever."

"No, Sam, what the doctor told you was that there was another option," he insisted. "Maybe you'll meet a guy you do want to go on this journey with, as you say."

She broke away from him, leaning forward to rest her elbows on her knees, scared she would blurt out some bitter sentiment, some resentful wish: *are you volunteering, Charlie Easter? Is there any chance in hell that you could have the staying power to go down this road with me? Would it ever be possible? Doubtful.*

She didn't turn to look at him, but spoke to her clenched fingers. "This is me letting it go, Charlie. I cannot have children. I have to accept that. Let me accept that."

He stroked the long hair cascading onto her shoulders. "Okay, I get it now."

She turned to face him and spoke slowly. "For so long, all I wanted was to have a baby. So what am I supposed to do now? Set a new goal or something? That just sounds silly."

"You're not supposed to do anything, Sam," he countered. "Take it easy. Give yourself time." He spread his arms and she melted into him. Her lips parted to welcome him in; his kiss was slow and lingering. He leaned back as she rested her forehead on his shoulder. "Can I stay tonight?" he asked.

"No," she said firmly.

He nodded. "Okay." He straightened his clothes, tugging on his white shirt. "Can I sleep in your atrium?" he asked.

"Charlie!" she exclaimed. "For crying out loud! I like this school! I'm passing for normal here!"

"What? What's the big deal? Nobody'd have to know, Sam."

"Oh, gee, Charlie. There were no secrets at Gertrude Stein Elementary years ago. I doubt this school is much different."

"Who knew we were together at Trudy's? Maybe a handful of people."

"Charlie, it was common knowledge you were sleeping in the school garden."

"I put in that garden for them there," he asserted with a touch of righteous indignation. "With my own time and money. They should have been grateful."

"Oh, my God!" She clasped her hands over her mouth and started to laugh.

"What, O'Malley? What is it now?"

"Nothing, just nothing."

"No, tell me—what?"

She rolled her eyes in embarrassed surrender. "Oh, I hate to admit this, but I missed you, God damn it. I hate you, but I missed you." He laughed and went to kiss her again, but she'd only allow a quick peck. "You've got to go, Mystery. It's late."

He stood and headed for the door. She followed slowly. "I'll see you tomorrow," he said.

She buried her face in her hands. "What—you're subbing at Rosa Parks again tomorrow? Jeez, will I never be rid of you?"

He embraced her, pulling her close, forehead to forehead. "You don't want to be rid of me."

She pulled away. "Get out of my house," she said with a satisfied cat grin. He smiled and floated out the door.

CHAPTER FOUR

She was running and panting, running like crazy in her bare feet. Her shoulders and hips were carrying her, turning like twin axles, propelling her hands and feet at a tremendous speed. It was white beneath her, white in front of her, white above her. She skidded to a halt, suddenly curious. What am I this time? She lifted a hand that was no longer a hand; it was a massive paw with thick white fur and enormous black claws. She gazed down at her belly, a forest of fur thicker than a shag carpet. She brushed a paw against her face. Hard to make out her features without the delicate touch of human fingers, but she had a snout, there was no mistaking her snout, and her round tufted ears. I'm a polar bear, she thought. She lifted her head to sniff the wind, it was strikingly cold, but she didn't care, in fact she felt energized in the cold. There was meat nearby, a seal or a deer of some kind. Hungry, so hungry. And then a flit of color, a yellow bill, black and white feathers. The magpie, it was the yellow-billed magpie again, flitting past her left ear, dashing by so fast, so warm, it left a streak of white fog in the air like the wake of a dolphin in water. She took after it, running fast, and then slipping, falling into the downy snow.

***

Samantha woke up feeling achy and irritable, wondering at her dream of snow as the radio announced a predicted high topping 100 degrees. She donned a light cotton dress but already felt sticky with sweat when she drove into the school parking lot. Charlie had just gotten out of his car and was heading toward her, an eager grin on his face. She gave him a warning glare and his expression turned sheepish. With obvious effort he extinguished his smile, then gave her a curt nod. "Ms O'Malley," he mumbled, all business.

"Good morning, Mr. Easter," she managed through clenched teeth. Then he gave her a quick wink and she felt herself blush.

Within minutes Samantha realized that this brief encounter with Charlie might well become the most pleasant event in her day. When she stepped into the stuffy classroom she discovered a message that Valerie would be out and Rose would be late. When the kids arrived she knew she'd need to distract them with busy work sheets since she could not run their usual work groups without assistants. But another issue concerned her. There were three doors in the room: one led outside toward the front of the school, the second connected with Bunny's classroom, and the third led to the school's auditorium. Alone without another adult, Samantha felt compelled to post sentries at each exit lest one of her stealthy "runners" dart out of the room. She seated reliable Aidan at the door to the street and chatty Ciera near the auditorium. She was wondering if she could safely leave the door to the other classroom unattended when Echo raised her hand and shouted out. "I can do it, teacher!" she cried. "Let me!"

Samantha regarded the girl keenly; after all Echo was the runner she was most worried about. "It's a big responsibility, Echo," she said seriously. "Do you really think you can handle it?"

Samantha expected Echo to bark out an insistence that she was up to the task, but Echo pursed her lips and stared at her fingers for a moment. Finally she looked up at Samantha. "I think I can do it, Ms O'Malley. I want to try."

Samantha was both amused and elated. "I'm so proud of you, Echo! I can see you gave this some thought. Go for it!" Echo beamed and scurried into position.

Thus fortified, she began an impromptu lesson on weather and maps, interspersed with chants and bursts of jumping jacks and "crab walk" races. When Rose arrived, pleading some undefined domestic emergency as the cause of her tardiness, the kids were still attentive, but Samantha was hot and bothered since the air conditioning hadn't kicked on. "I'll take care of that," Rose said and she pulled a small hair dryer out from the back of a low-lying cabinet. Samantha lifted an eyebrow.

"Give me a minute," Rose said, so Samantha led the class in a rousing rendition of "This Land is My Land." Rose plugged in and pointed the hot air at the thermostat.

"Please tell me this isn't typical," Samantha said.

Rose shrugged. "In winter we press blue ice packs against the thermostat until the heat comes on."

The AC finally blasted through and the two women called the kids to work groups.

Samantha was so proud of Echo that she decided to push the envelope further. While Aidan, Billy, and Tony were quietly writing their names and addresses on mock job applications, Samantha laid out some cards she used with Luisa for Echo to see. "This is called the Picture Exchange Communication System or PECS. You've seen me use these with Lulu. Now I would love it if you could use them to work with Lulu too, while I'm helping other kids. I think it would be fun for you."

Echo fingered one of the cards and gave Samantha a skeptical glare. "This is what you think is fun?"

Samantha burst out laughing at the girl's unaffected bluntness. Lulu squealed and Samantha squeezed her shoulders to calm her. "Well," she mused, pointedly looking at Echo, "I actually do think working with Lulu is fun, but I see your point." The teacher and child exchanged wry glances, each apparently satisfied that they understood each other a bit better now. Samantha gave Lulu some crayons and paper to scribble on, then she turned again to Echo.

"Look, sweetie, I want you to think about this. I need help and Lulu needs help. You need help too! I don't know if it will be fun, but I hope it will make you feel proud because you'll be making a difference in someone's life. It would also make your mom happy to know that you're making a good choice like this."

Echo twisted a lock of hair around her finger. "I guess I could try," she conceded.

"Just think about it now, and we'll talk more later," Samantha promised. She gave Echo a worksheet to complete, then she turned to see how the boys were doing. Billy and Tony were still writing, but Aidan, reliably compliant Aidan, had put down his pencil. He had taken off his right shoe and was gnawing on his big toenail. Sam's eyes popped open. What a limber child! She pulled a page from her ever-present notebook and scrawled a quick note to Aidan's mother. "Aidan has indicated that his toe nails are in need of clipping," she wrote.

"Put your shoes on your feet and put this note in your backpack," she told Aidan. "Almost time for recess, and not a minute too soon."

Samantha called her students one at a time to line up while Rose retrieved sunglasses and floppy hat from the locked cabinet in the back. She praised the hard work they'd done this morning, and the maturity they'd shown to help her when she was alone before Rose arrived. Just then Ciera, a stocky girl with a stylish pixie hair cut, standing at the front of the line, reached into the back of her stretchy spandex shorts to scratch her backside, exposing more than half her crack, effectively mooning the entire class. "Ciera!" Samantha shouted, finally blowing her patient demeanor. "We don't do that!"

The children joined in Samantha's scold with a chorus of ew's and laughter. Ciera opened her mouth and grimaced like a spitting cat. "I got an itch," she shouted back at Samantha in a matter of fact way. The shouts and giggles grew louder.

Samantha moved quickly to the door where she could flip the light switch off and then back on again. She gave the children the full on teacher stare. "I'm waiting," she said softly. The children calmed themselves fast, aware this was eating their recess time. "Look," Samantha said in a low voice, "This goes for all of you: if you have an itch in a private spot you go somewhere private like the bathroom before you can scratch." She paused. Their faces looked solemn. "And," she continued slowly for emphasis, "if there's no private place where you can go, then you live with the itch!"

"Gross," Ciera said and the snickers began again.

Samantha tapped her wristwatch. "I've got all day," she said, and the kids quieted themselves again. Samantha and Rose exchanged satisfied nods and the aide led them out of the room.

***

At the end of the day, Samantha was making her usual trip out to the bus, Luisa in tow. As she rounded the corner to head toward the traffic circle, Luisa squealed and bounced her free hand off her open mouth, as if giving a loud warrior cry. She stopped in her tracks and jumped up and down, as if she had springs on the bottoms of her feet.

Samantha draped her arm around Luisa, afraid she might run off, but Luisa continued to gyrate. "What's up, Lulu?" Samantha asked. "We've got to get to the bus, sweetie."

Lulu seemed as frantic and strong as a skittish deer. As hot and tired as she was, Samantha worried that she would be unable to contain the girl. She looked around seeking a staff member to help.

Then Samantha caught sight of two women strolling up from the parking lot. They were both large women, majestically tall with big hips like beautiful Clydesdale horses. One was young, early 20s with honey colored hair; the older was perhaps 50 with hair the color of dark chocolate. They waved and called Luisa's name. "She's calling to us!" the older said to Samantha. "I'm Luisa's mother." She extended her hand. "Anna Villaseñor."

Samantha smiled in relief. "Oh, so good to meet you." She released Luisa, and the girl fell against her mother's chest, pushing her open mouth against the woman's raw silk blouse. Anna laughed gleefully at her daughter's exuberant greeting, seemingly undisturbed that her daughter was drooling all over a very expensive fabric. Anna Villaseñor immediately ascended in Samantha's esteem.

Anna pointed her chin toward her young companion. "This is Luisa's nanny, Jessica."

The younger woman extended her hand and exchanged greetings with Samantha. "It's so very good to meet you, Ms O'Malley," she said formally. For such a tall young woman, she had a surprisingly high voice.

Anna rocked Luisa affectionately until the girl calmed and stopped squealing. Jessica put her arm around Luisa and gently pulled her away. Samantha observed that this seemed to be a practiced routine, and hoped she'd have a chance to learn more from this parent. Anna seemed to be reading her mind. She looked at the teacher pointedly. "I know we've come by unexpectedly; I had a staff meeting this afternoon that had to be cancelled because my lead manager was ill. At any rate, I was hoping for an opportunity to speak with you. Of course if this isn't a good time, I'd be happy to schedule something for your convenience."

"Actually this is a great time," Samantha said. "Let's all head back to our classroom."

"Jessica and I have come in separate vehicles," Anna said authoritatively. "She and Luisa will head home. I'll be needed back at my office within the hour, but I think that will give us a small window of time to get acquainted."

"Of course." Samantha could see that Anna was a take-charge kind of woman. She was both impressed and nervous. She'd spent many years in an inner city school district working with parents who had lived in refugee camps or worked as migrants picking crops in the central valley. These business types who were buying up the McMansions in the upscale new subdivisions left her in awe.

She surreptitiously eyed Anna as they strolled back to the classroom. Anna was a portly woman but she carried herself gracefully. Her long hair was swept into a bun like a crown resting on top of her head. Her fingernails were carefully manicured and painted a subtle but dark pinkish brown. Everything about her seemed polished and refined. After a day of watching kids chew their toenails and scratch their butts, Samantha felt as if she'd entered a separate dimension.

In the classroom, Samantha felt obliged to put on a little show, like a docent or tour guide. She was proud of the work she'd done to decorate the room to make it colorful and age-appropriate. She knew many special ed classrooms looked like kindergartens no matter what the age of the students. It was true the children were still working on some developmental tasks but the room reflected a home for 9 to 11-year-olds. A "favorite things" wall dominated a back corner, where the kids had been allowed to hang clipped photos of wrestlers, TV stars and superheroes. Maps and posters of Native American tribes, California missions, the state capitol and Sutter's Fort indicated the class was studying the 4th grade California history curriculum.

"Here's Luisa's desk," Samantha said in a perfunctory tone.

"We've seated her near a few girls who are good helpers. They're eager to help Luisa at lunch and recess time, and to teach her to pay attention and stay with the group."

Anna nodded. "These other girls are also on the spectrum?"

"Oh," Samantha said quickly, unprepared for the question. "Well uh, it wouldn't be appropriate for me to discuss other students' diagnoses with you. I can tell you that all the students in this class have severe disabilities, but not all are identified as being on the autism spectrum." She took a deep breath satisfied she had given a polished response as she pointed Anna toward a table and chairs.

"I was curious about that," Anna said, her voice low and well modulated, as she sat across from Samantha. "I wasn't sure if Luisa was in a class that was strictly reserved for students with Autism Spectrum Disorder, or whether there was a variety of special needs in this classroom."

"We're a small district," Samantha noted, affecting a reserved, monotonous beat to match her tone to the other woman's. "We need to serve all intermediate-aged students with severe disabilities in this one class."

Anna slipped off her sunglasses and hit Samantha with a penetrating gaze. "Do you think that's the best philosophy?" she asked.

Samantha lowered her chin to return Anna look. "I've always believed in heterogeneous groupings," she said. "It gives the higher functioning kids classmates that they can help: that's great for their self esteem. And it gives the lower functioning kids better role models. That's key--I truly do believe that."

Anna gave a sharp nod. "You make a good case," she said curtly, though she didn't sound convinced as she opened her large Coach bag, extracted her sunglass case, and folded her glasses neatly away. She looked up abruptly. "Tell me how Luisa is doing generally," she commanded as if she were chairing a board meeting.

Samantha was startled by Anna's tone, but she cleared her throat, determined to sound casual and undefensive. "Oh, Luisa is fine," she responded. "We're making some progress on the goals that were written in the last placement—where was it? I've forgotten—the east bay?"

"Yes, we moved over the summer from Danville. We're enjoying it here. It's too hot of course, but we're meeting lovely people. At any rate, you say, she's making progress?"

"Yes," Samantha confirmed. "I feel like she's had a bit of a break-through with the picture exchange communication system. Just this week she's started asking us for M&M's at snack time. We were excited."

"Well, I don't want to sound discouraging," Anna said, "but she was doing that at the Diagnostic Center in Danville."

Samantha was undaunted. "Yes, I read that in the file, but this is the first time she's done it here. That's shows generalization—an understanding that the skill can cross domains and be applicable in different settings." Samantha felt herself blush. Under this microscope she was resorting to professional speak, exclusionary lingo. She didn't like herself right now; she felt she was being forced to perform.

But Anna was nodding. "I see what you mean; that is significant. I have to admit that Luisa doesn't use the PECS icons at home. Okay, I should say she seldom uses them with me. Jessica guides her through her exercises with them at snack and play time. But you know--" She paused for a moment. Her next words came slowly, her eyes downcast. "At the end of a long day, I don't want to work to communicate with my daughter. I make a point of being home for dinner most nights, and I just want to visit with her while we're sharing food. Sometimes more of her food ends up on the floor and tablecloth, and even in my lap, but that's okay. I just want to enjoy being with her." She looked up at Samantha. "I won't apologize for that."

Samantha exhaled, grateful for this window of candor. "Well you certainly don't need to apologize to me! Both you and Luisa are entitled to down time, when you just get to be together. I think that's great."

Anna grinned. "I knew I was going to like you, Samantha. I

could tell from the little newsletter you sent home. Very personable." She pulled her shoulders back and returned to her business-like demeanor. "At any rate, I need to go now. My assistant will be paging me any minute, so I better get on the road." She pulled her car keys from a compartment in her massive purse. "I promise this is going to change. I want to be more involved in Luisa's class. When the new shop is open next week, I'll have more time."

"The new shop?" Samantha asked softly.

For a moment Anna looked deflated, a celebrity who had not been recognized. "I'm sorry; I thought you knew. I'm Anna Victoria—of Anna Victoria's Pies. I have six shops in the bay area, one in Roseville, and now the new one at 48th and H Streets. My grandfather used to be a gardener who serviced a dozen different mansions between 39th and J and 52nd and M—up and down the Fab Forties." She tapped Samantha's hand. "You know the Fab Forties, don't you?"

Samantha laughed, tapping Anna's hand in return. "Every Sacramentan knows that area from 40th to 50th Streets," Samantha agreed. "You know the Reagans lived there when he was governor."

"Indeed I do know," Anna said. "And now I'm the dessert maven in those blocks." She pulled out her maroon rimmed sunglasses again, gesturing dramatically with them as she placed them over her brown eyes. "I'm proud of that."

"You should be!"

"Have you tried my pies?" Anna asked eagerly.

"I'm sorry to say that I haven't. I've heard they're fabulous."

"What's your favorite kind of pie?" Anna persisted.

"Oh, I like most anything." Samantha paused to give her waist a comical pinch. "Unfortunately, I've never been a picky eater."

Anna lowered her glasses to give her a mock glare. "Not even a hint, huh? Well, I'll just have to surprise you. And I will. When you least expect it."

Samantha licked her dry lips. "It's not necessary--" she began.

"It's never necessary," Anna conceded. "But I wouldn't have built a successful business with an attitude like that! Like I said— when you least expect it."

***

Samantha sat at the table, entering the data she had jotted in her notebook throughout the day into each child's folder. Tony was making progress learning to count a combination of nickels and pennies, and Ciera was finally starting to count pennies without skipping every third or fourth one. Lisa had the last two digits of her phone number memorized, and Billy was finally writing his first name with two l's.

She came to Luisa's folder and paused, staring into space. Anna was a powerhouse; there was no denying that. *Did it take that kind of gravitas to adopt a child,* Samantha wondered, *or could someone as insecure as I am brave single motherhood too?* Of course Anna had a staff, a large staff apparently, to help out at home, at the office and at her pie shops. Samantha had a cat. She laughed softly to herself. Was she crazy to even think of adopting a child? She tapped her pen on the table. Crazy or not, she would consider it--or rather, she would pray about it.

A thump on the door beat out "shave and a hair cut—two bits"— and Samantha had to smile again. "Come in," she called, and the door cautiously cracked open. Charlie stuck his head inside "M'lady," he said with a bow, "tis your humble servant."

"Get in here before someone sees you acting like an ass," she giggled. She took a deep breath. She was treading on thin ice allowing this man-child back into her life, but she hadn't had this much fun in years. Undoubtedly there would be hell to pay.

"Got plans for tonight?" he asked. "We could go to Willie's— remember the onion rings at Willie's?"

"A girl could get fat hanging out with you, Mystery."

"You need some flesh on those bones, girl." He squeezed her knee as he sunk into the chair beside her. "You don't have much to hang onto."

She gave him a gentle back handed swipe on his shoulder. "I've got too much work to catch up on this afternoon, Charlie. Then I just want to go home, take a cool bath."

"Can I come over and watch?"

"I'm so tired I can't even come up with a smart-assed retort to that."

"In that case," he began.

"The answer is no. Definitely no."

He laughed. "Can't blame a guy for trying."

He stood up and she looked at him for a long moment, feeling disappointed he had given up so easily. "You got somewhere else you're going?" she asked.

He looked confused. "I don't know. Probably."

She stared at her hands. She knew him. He was never one to rush home at quitting time. He liked to visit old friends or meet new ones. He liked to go for a run or a swim or a tour of an art gallery.

He dropped back into the chair beside her. "Something wrong?"

She looked up from her notebook and files. "I guess I was wondering--"

"What?"

She put down her pen. "I was wondering if there was someone else—you know—that you were going to go see."

Charlie laughed. "Oh, Ms Omm! You got the Mystery for one short evening, and already you're demanding monogamy."

"I did not say that!" she exclaimed indignantly. "I just--"

"'You just!'" he mocked, still grinning.

Feeling embarrassed, she stood up and retreated to her desk in the corner. "Whatever, Charlie."

"No, Sam, I'm sorry. What were you going to say?"

Her mouth fell open, and for a moment she didn't know if she would burst into tears or laughter. "I don't know, Charlie. It's just that it's been less than two month since I left my husband. And here you are again—here *we* are again. It's a little overwhelming."

He stood and stepped toward her, then took her hands in his. "It's overwhelming for me too."

She shook her head. "The difference, Charlie Easter, is that you like it when a big old ocean wave knocks you into the surf. Me—I'm more of a 'let me spread out my beach towel so I can read my paperback novel in the sun' kind of girl. I'm not looking for no tsunami."

He touched her hair. "So let me give you some space tonight, Sam." He started to step away, but she gripped his hand tight. "What?" he asked.

"You are flirting with me big time, Mystery, and I have a right to know: are you seeing anybody else?"

He shook his head. "No, there's nobody else."

She nodded and pulled her hands away. "Okay."

They stood awkward for a moment. Samantha picked up papers from her desk and stooped to file them.

"Hey," Charlie said, boisterously breaking the silence, "the least I can do is get you a lousy candy bar from the machine in the staff room. What'll it be—Snickers or peanut butter cups?"

She tipped back her head. "I hate that you know everything about me!"

"No problem!-- you want a surprise? I can surprise you. Give me a minute." He dug into his right hip pocket as he headed for the door to the auditorium. "You know, I think I'm a quarter short. . ."

"No surprise there," she said whimsically.

"Wait, I've got some extra dimes. I'm good, O'Malley, so stop your beefing." He turned abruptly. "Would it be quicker to the office this way?" he asked, indicating the door through Bunny's room.

"Six of one," Samantha said.

"No, I think this will be quicker." He pushed forcefully on the door, and a woman screamed. Charlie jumped back in surprise. He stepped forward and opened the door slowly this time. "Mrs. Schwartz?" he blurted. "Are you okay?"

"I'm fine," the husky throated woman said as she scurried away. "I just need some Kleenex."

"Are you sure you're okay?" he asked. "It looks like your nose is bleeding!"

"I'm fine!" she repeated harshly.

Charlie pulled the door closed and leaned against it. He stared at Samantha meaningfully. "I think the walls have ears, Sam," he whispered.

She nodded knowingly. "Bunny ears," she whispered.

There was a sharp rap at the front door. "Now what?" Charlie said, spreading his arms wide. "This room is like Grand Central Station."

Samantha came around from behind her desk to accompany him to this door. "It's you, Easter. You're perpetual motion and like attracts like."

She opened the door. An Asian teen in a teal-colored polo shirt stood at the threshold with a matching teal-colored box tied with pink string. "Ms O'Malley?" he asked.

"Yes?"

"I'm Adam Yang; I work for Anna Victoria." He thrust the box toward her. "White chocolate apricot pie: a grand opening special."

"Wow," Samantha said in awe as she accepted the box. "Thank you."

"When you least expect it," the young man said. "Ms Villaseñor wanted you to know."

CHAPTER FIVE

A week passed, and Samantha did not see Charlie. She heard from him though: he had taken to tweeting her. She found this amusing since she had seldom made use of the twitter account herself. It was something Tom's campaign manager insisted she acquire during Tom's reelection bid. The campaign assigned an aide to send out tweets in her name—benign notes of gratitude to those who held fund raisers and hosted dinners, the occasional exuberant encouragement for voters to check out a fascinating article or link. But back then all this was happening right in the middle of fertility treatments. Reading the cheery tweets from @SamJan often left Samantha seeking an anxious grip on her own identity. SamJan seemed to be a pleasant person and a happy person. Samantha was undisputedly not SamJan; she had never even taken Tom's last name. But could she pretend to be SamJan? Did she want to actually be SamJan?

She had met Tom at a Very Special Arts Exhibit and fundraiser held at the State Fairgrounds featuring the work of students from all over northern California. The place was lousy with politicians and local radio and TV personalities. She was with a cluster of parents sipping sparkling apple juice and showing off her class's paintings of colorful rain forest macaws when Tom happened by. He was fresh off his first election to the county board of supervisors. She thought he was cocky. But she was still stinging from her break-up with Charlie and the death of her father. His attention was a salve to her wounded psyche.

The real attraction was the fact that Tom was the type of guy Samantha had never been able to attract: tall, athletic, good-looking, and jeez louise!-- popular. She felt like she was back in high school and the student body president had asked her to prom. It was a taste of something she'd never had and hadn't realized she'd been craving.

When they would arrive at a formal dinner/fund raiser/ribbon cutting-type-event, Samantha felt so pretty in the new dresses and shoes and jewelry Tom had bought for her. When reporters lobbed her some softball question, she would respond with gratitude to the taxpayers and donors for the new library books or playground equipment or park fountain, and people would cheer for her. It was such heady stuff.

But when they went home Samantha was bored. Tom was intelligent, but he wasn't an intellectual: he had no interest in novels, poetry, history or art. He went to church with her, but he wasn't spiritual: he had no desire to meditate or pray with her or discuss philosophy. Samantha blamed herself. She'd been caught in a whirlwind and married too fast, before she'd really gotten to know her husband. Yet he was sincere in his efforts to please her and generous to a fault. He made it clear he would get her anything she wanted: clothes, jewelry, trips around the world. If she wanted a baby, he would make it happen even if he had to buy another woman's uterus to incubate their progeny, even if he had to personally travel to a third world country and buy a baby on the black market. Anything.

Before long Samantha realized what she wanted from Tom was the good grace to allow her to slink back to the valley quietly. She wanted nothing more than to be Samantha O'Malley in jeans and a t-shirt again.

Now Charlie Easter had discovered the @SamJan account, still linked as it was to her email box. He sent her updates at least once, usually two or three times a day. He was subbing at a school on the other side of the freeway, and he sent her a daily photograph of restaurant meals he was sampling on this side of the district. "Desperately seeking non-chain food," he'd tweet daily. "No luck yet, but this looks good."

"mmmm, mmmm, good. . ." Samantha dutifully responded each day.

She felt a bit of wicked glee that any followers of @T-Jan and @SamJan might be noticing these public online exchanges. Yet she took care to send conservative tweets that responded to Charlie's inquiries about work and health, but also inform Tom's public of her new status.

"So proud of my students: very attentive in assembly!"

"Great day for my girl E. Good job helping her friend Lu!"

"Enjoying warm valley weather. Will start new garden Sat."

Then one day the T-Jan account came to life, dropping hints that Tom was dating the pretty young librarian that Samantha used to help out once or twice a week. Samantha clicked to open a photo attached to the tweet. The librarian was tall, close to Tom's height in fact. They made an attractive couple. Samantha was surprised to feel a pang of jealousy. The librarian was at least ten years younger than she was. Certainly she had plenty of childbearing years ahead of her. With a crazy mixture of resentment and relief, she "unfollowed" T-Jan.

She quickly moved to open Charlie's account and noted his usual lunchtime tweet. She wondered why Charlie didn't suggest getting together, but maybe he was waiting for a sign from her. She had to admit to herself that she didn't know what she wanted. Have I ever made a plan or set goals for myself? she wondered. Or have I allowed life to blow me around like a feather in the wind? And what if I have? Is there anything wrong with that?

Sitting at her desk at lunchtime, she glanced at her cell phone, tempted to pick it up and tweet that sentiment right now. "Am I nothing more than a feather in the wind?" But instead she stood up and slid the phone into her pocket. She headed over to the staff room. She wanted to get to know her co-workers better.

***

At the end of the day, Samantha stood at the back of the room near the door to the street, prompting her students to remember homework and parental notes. Through the window she spied Echo's mother Sally, baby Phoebe at her hip, waiting for dismissal. Samantha leaned toward the window and gave Sally a smiling thumbs-up. Sally's eyes widened in surprise and she returned Samantha's upbeat gesture.

When Samantha met Echo's mother she was surprised to

discover she liked the young woman. She had ash blonde hair, a butterfly tattooed on her throat, and a row of studs in her ears and eyebrow. But she was vulnerable and sweet, and she wanted nothing more than for Echo to have a good day. "This is the most nerve-racking fifteen minutes of my day," she confessed to Samantha the first week of school. "I get so nervous walking over here, wondering if she's been good or not, wondering what our evening will be like." She smiled but she looked like she might cry.

Sally was not the mom Samantha had expected her to be. Echo's school file bulged with reports, spinning a story of violence and manipulation. Echo had been bounced from foster home to foster home, while Sally was serving a prison sentence for manufacturing butane hash oil.

The week before school started, Samantha had called the girl's former teacher. The unseen woman sounded shrill. "I feel sorry for you," she had told Samantha, "but I'm sure glad she's out of my hair. That girl is bad news. You know, she stabbed her own aunt. Did her mother tell you that?"

Samantha drew in a sharp breath, then coughed to remain calm. "I haven't met her mother yet," she said.

"Well, let me tell you: nearly every day Echo would throw a tantrum and rip papers and posters off the wall. It was awful. That girl cannot be controlled. She does it on purpose. We tried putting her into the 5th grade class for time-out but she liked it in there, so I had to stop."

Maybe you should have made her earn some time in the 5th grade classroom if she liked it so much, Samantha thought, but she said nothing. She just listened.

"She was living with her aunt because no foster home would have her—she was that unmanageable." Samantha rested her head in her hands as she listened to the other teacher rant. She had entered the realm of hyperbole, and Samantha would no longer be able to trust what she said. "Then she tried to kill her aunt, so they had to let her mother out of prison because she was the only one Echo wouldn't harm. That mother must have a heart of stone to put up with that child."

"I just need to know if you've got a psych report on her," Samantha said. "A current one."

"Our psychologists are overwhelmed with kids who need to be tested," the teacher said in a haughty tone. "We have real problems over here," she continued. "We have huge pockets of poverty in south Sacramento. We don't have all those brand new lovely McMansions filled with cybertech engineers and professional basketball players."

Samantha sighed. When she was younger, she would have told this woman off. But she used to work for that school district too, and she was given very little support, neither from administration nor union. She was sure that this teacher, this Mrs. Miller, must be frustrated and angry. But she was wrong about Samantha's new employer. As Samantha was quickly learning, this district was not a plush upper middle class enclave. South of the freeway the neighborhoods consisted of decades-old tract housing and run-down apartment complexes. North of the freeway, sure, there were plenty of new luxury condos and three story houses with six car garages. But a huge percentage of the people that "owned" those were upside down in their mortgages. Tough times had arrived, and they weren't leaving anytime soon.

Samantha had finally interrupted her. "Thank you for your time, Mrs. Miller," she said briefly, and then she had hung up on her.

The kids were lined up, not perfectly, but good enough. Samantha opened the door slowly, allowing Rose to lead them to the bus. Valerie brought up the rear, firmly holding Lulu's hand.

Samantha grinned at Sally. "Echo was a great helper today!" she announced triumphantly. "She most certainly earned the Wii tonight!"

"You were a helper?" Sally eagerly asked her daughter.

"Yeah," Echo drawled as she rocked back and forth in her frayed running shoes. "I helped Lulu with her cards. It wasn't fun," she added pointedly, "but Lulu seemed to like it."

Samantha smirked at Echo's description. "We'll have to talk about ways to make it more fun for you," she told the girl.

"Not everything can be fun, sweetheart," Sally scolded. "Don't be a smart mouth."

Samantha tapped Sally's arm. "It's okay, Sally. She followed directions! She did a great job! And I hope she'll help me again tomorrow."

"Oh, I'm sure she will!" Sally exclaimed anxiously. "You will, won't you?" Sally said, her brow furrowed.

"Hey," Samantha said, interrupting again. "Let's just celebrate today! You were amazing today, Echo."

Echo smiled shyly and gave Samantha a high five. She turned to her mother. "Can I hold Phoebe?" she asked. Sally released the baby to the older girl's care. Laughing and cooing, Echo walked her sister to the nearby lawn.

Samantha lowered her voice. "Sally, don't worry so much! Echo had a great day. Let go of tomorrow for now. Focus on praising and rewarding Echo this evening and tomorrow will take care of itself."

"But she was rude to you just now," Sally lamented, "saying it wasn't fun--"

"Maybe," Samantha conceded, "but she was being honest. Look, I gave her a job above and beyond her regular work. If I want her to help Lulu on a regular basis, I need to make it fun or it will be another struggle for both Echo and me."

Sally shook her head. "Wow, you're so patient!"

Samantha resisted an urge to roll her eyes: she'd gotten that compliment often enough whether she deserved it or not. "Sometimes I'm patient," Samantha said, "but for the most part it's a matter of having reasonable expectations. You know, baby steps."

Sally nodded. "I do know. One Day At A Time," she recited in a practiced cadence.

Samantha nodded sympathetically, picturing Sally sitting in a church hall on a folding chair, drinking coffee from a Styrofoam cup, sharing stories with the group. *I have no idea,* she thought, *no way I can imagine, how hard her life must be.* She forced a smile of encouragement, suddenly struck by the thought that perhaps her childless state was a blessing rather than a curse. She would be happy to return to a quiet house this evening. "One day at a time," she agreed lamely. "That's the right idea."

"You've been so good to me," Sally gushed. "Is there something I can do for you? Something to help out?"

"Well, if you're interested," Samantha said brightly, "the PTA is starting a new volunteer brigade. I could sign you up if you like. It'll give you a chance to meet a lot of people in the community."

"That would be nice," Sally said nodding eagerly. "I'd like to help any way I can."

"Now the first thing you need to do is go down to the district office and be fingerprinted, and then you have to get a TB test. It's just a formality. All of us who work for the school district have to do this, and now volunteers do too. Like I said, just a formality."

"Oh." Sally dropped her gaze down to the concrete and her lip quivered. "I don't know if I can do that." She paused. "You know—oh, I'm so embarrassed, but I did do time in prison—it wasn't very long—for drug possession. That's why I lost Echo. I don't know if I could pass this 'formality.'"

"Oh, well, I don't know either," Samantha said considering. "Let me talk to our principal. I'm sure he can give us some guidance."

***

Samantha knocked on the principal's open door. "Jon," she said. "I need to talk to you. Is this a good time?"

Jon pushed away from his computer and turned to face Samantha. "Sure," he said, gesturing toward a chair in front of his desk.

"Thanks," Samantha said, and she closed the door behind her, signaling that the topic was confidential. He sat up in his chair a little straighter. "What can I do for you?"

"It's about the parent of one of my students—Echo's mom," Samantha began. "You know she has a sketchy past, but she tries so hard. She comes over here nearly every day to walk Echo home, and she's been so supportive of everything we do in the classroom. She even backs up the behavior support plan we've got for Echo. She has rewards for Echo at home if she's had a good day here. She's very sincere."

"So what does she need?" Jon asked.

"Well, she'd like to do some volunteer work here at the school; I think it would be so good for her to meet the other parents. But I know the district has this new directive that everyone has be fingerprinted—even if they're not going to work directly with the kids."

"That's state law now," he noted.

"I know, and it's a good precaution of course. But in this case—well, she told me she has a prison record, so she's concerned that she won't be allowed to volunteer here. I was wondering if we could look into it."

Jon took a deep breath and scratched his head. "What was she in prison for, Samantha?"

"Drugs," she said briefly.

He stared at her, waiting for more details. This Zen-like silence seemed to be the basis of his management technique. In the brief few weeks they'd worked together Samantha had seen him pull out this trick at meetings, sitting quietly, his face expectant, until other people took responsibility to throw out ideas and eventually even volunteered to take on additional duties. At that point Jon would swoop in to lock in decisions made and action agreed to. It was impressive, but so far she had managed to sidestep the power of his silence. She stared back at him.

"Drugs," he said finally, repeating her statement. He was good. She had to nod.

"I don't know the whole story, but Echo's previous teacher told me it was cannabis." She paused, and he dropped his chin, apparently surprised at her formality. Still he said nothing. She shifted in her chair. "Well, I guess she and Echo's father were actually making hash oil. You know, butane hash oil. That can be a rather dangerous occupation."

Jon leaned back, shaking his head. "That's pretty serious stuff."

"Yes," Samantha said quickly, "but it's not child abuse, it's not child molestation. I mean—that's what they're looking for with the finger printing, isn't it? She's not a pedophile—at most the charge against her would have been child endangerment!"

Jon gazed at her, his eyebrows raised, half a smile playing on his lips. She looked at him, and they sat this way for several seconds. Finally she burst out laughing. He laughed too. "I just heard myself," she said. "I just heard what I said." She paused to catch her breath. "Oh, poor Sally, she really does try hard. I really think she's worked hard to get Echo back. She's left Echo's father, she has a new baby with her fiancée. Sometimes Echo's new stepbrother comes by to pick her up, to walk her home—and gee, what a nice kid. He's probably 15 or 16, and he's so polite. I just think that's got to be a good sign, a good reflection on his father—Echo's new stepfather. You know what I mean?"

Jon leaned back in his chair and smiled at her. He had a whimsical, elf-like smile that crinkled his eyes, cheeks and jawline. "Samantha, it's delightful to see a teacher like yourself who still has faith in people. Most people would write off someone like Echo and her family. I'm glad you're willing to give her a chance."

"But. . ." Samantha said in a leading tone as if anticipating his next words.

"Well, you already know what I'm going to say, Samantha," he said. "I'm sure with a record like that, Mrs. Abernathy won't be able to get approval to do volunteer work. I'm afraid not."

She shrugged. "I can see that."

"And you have to realize that this protects all of us—you most of all," he pointed out. "What if she doesn't live up to the trust you place in her? You make yourself liable when you give her your seal of approval."

Samantha felt a bit embarrassed and could feel her cheeks

warm. "I guess I sound rather naïve."

"Not necessarily naïve," he interjected quickly. "Just open to possibility."

Samantha glanced down at her hands, resisting an urge to deny Jon's compliment. Open to possibility? Well, that certainly sounded like SamJan! But denim-clad Samantha O'Malley, special ed teacher and valley-dweller, was feeling rather jaded lately. "I guess," she said slowly, "it's nice to be reminded that I can still be open-minded once in a while."

"It's difficult in this business not to get hardened. Don't lose that beginner's mind. Obviously, you haven't—or you wouldn't have come in here in the first place."

She smiled and nodded, but she felt a little bad, as if she had put on a sheepskin and was misrepresenting herself. Wasn't she really a hungry wolf, frantically seeking sustenance? She stood up and reached for the doorknob. "Thanks, Jon."

"You know, Samantha," he said before she could go, "if Echo's mom wants to meet other parents in the community, she might come to the parenting classes the district will be holding soon—I think they're slated to begin in November."

"That's a good idea. I'll tell her."

"And Samantha—don't take on problems that don't belong to you."

She frowned. "What do you mean?"

"I mean this woman has already chosen a hard road for herself—that's not your fault," he cautioned. "Don't let her pull you into her drama."

"Oh, she hasn't," she said.

"You have a big heart," he continued. "Leave some room in there for yourself."

"Okay," she said feeling confused. "Okay, thanks."

She walked into the hallway, nearly running into the far wall to avoid three fifth graders running through. "Slow down," she heard Jon yell at the kids behind her. She smiled at him, but kept walking, worried that he seemed to feel she needed protecting. She squared her shoulders, hoping she looked capable of carrying a heavy load

CHAPTER SIX

Another week passed. Samantha sat at the table near the door to the auditorium eating a fruit salad at lunchtime. She could hear Bunny and her class on the other side of her back door loudly chanting something about poodles and noodles and oodles of fun.

She took a deep breath, closed her eyes and tried to focus on the sweetness of a white peach in her mouth. So fresh and good.

"Wait a minute," Bunny's husky voice rang out. "You stop that right now! I see what you're doing! Why, you little brat! You will not get away with that. Not in *my* classroom!"

The door near Samantha's right hand swung open and Charlie burst in. "Hey, Ms Omm," he blurted with a grin.

Samantha turned to him wild-eyed, her hand raised like a stop sign. "Hush," she hissed in a stage whisper. She swung her arm around to point at the other door. Charlie froze.

"You may do that at home," Bunny continued to scream. "But not here! Not on my watch!"

Samantha's gaze shifted to Charlie's face. His eyebrows were pressed down and his eyes were lowered. His mouth was drawn in a thin line. He seemed far away, unaware of her.

"Oh, now, don't you cry," Bunny yelled even louder than before. "You know what you did. You just go to your desk and put your head down. You ought to be ashamed. Go on!"

Samantha shifted her weight and looked back down at her salad as Bunny's voice seemed to grow distant. She could hear the click of Bunny's boots on the linoleum. She was apparently moving the kids to the other side of the room.

Charlie looked up and glanced at her, then lowered himself into a chair beside her. He was subdued now, cheerful mood gone.

"She yells at those little kids like that nearly every day," Samantha said softly. "What could a 5-year-old possibly do that she should be ashamed?"

Charlie shrugged. "She sounds like my mother," he said.

Samantha stared at him stunned, but he looked down at his hands. He looked up abruptly. "So how's your day?" he exclaimed, big display of bravado.

Samantha clenched her teeth, suddenly remembering this about Charlie, the way he would reveal some tantalizing tidbit from his past, like a fan dancer flashing an intimate piece of flesh, then he'd back off, buttoning up again with a boisterous change of subject. She wanted to confront him: be who you are! Trust me to accept you, to love you. But they were at work. A student could burst through the door any minute: no time for confidences now. She reached for his hand. "My day is going well," she said. "I didn't know you were here. PE again?"

"No, I've got Jean Moss's fourth grade. Nice group, well behaved."

The phone rang on Samantha's desk and Charlie rose. "Let me get it."

Samantha drew in a quick breath, unsure if she wanted anyone to find out Charlie was visiting her at lunchtime, but she fought the urge to race him to the phone. "Ms O'Malley's room." He sounded very professional. She sighed. She felt silly.

"Okay, sure—I could come up. Oh, well, even better. That's fine."

He hung up. "A gift has arrived for you, Ms Omm." He looked pensive, but also whimsical. "So—you got a new boyfriend? Is he sending you flowers, perhaps?"

She opened her mouth, ready to blurt out a denial, then she

stopped herself, deciding to tease him. "I can't imagine which of my many paramours…"

A sharp rap on the door stopped her. She took another bite of her salad. "Could you get that, Mr. Easter?" she asked politely.

"My pleasure."

At the door was Adam Yang with a pale yellow shirt and a box to match. "French pear," he said ceremoniously. "Ms Villaseñor says she'll be by to visit tomorrow."

***

Samantha chose her clothing carefully the next morning, wanting to look her professional best. She wore sleek oyster colored trousers, a navy blue shell and jacket. She slipped on navy pumps and her mother's Clauddaugh earrings. She pulled her hair back, and she applied her nighttime lipstick. She hadn't had that color out since the last catered dinner party in the foothills. She studied herself in the mirror, then wiped the lipstick off. Cherry flavored chapstick was good enough for everyday. It would have to be good enough for Anna Villaseñor too.

Anna arrived promptly, fifteen minutes after the buses had left, when the children were gone for the day. She was dressed in a utilitarian black pantsuit, but a flashy floral scarf with fuchsia and yellow streaks graced her shoulders like a shawl. She looked radiant with smoky eyes and red lipstick. Samantha pressed her chapstick embalmed lips together, grateful for the moisture.

"A colleague faxed me this article last week," Anna told Samantha as she pulled a folder out of her oversized pink purse. She spread the papers on the table between them. "This young girl— Miranda, her name is—she's autistic like Luisa. They've been training her with Applied Behavior Analysis techniques, but then, one day, she started to type. Just sat down and started to type. Have you heard about this?"

Samantha swallowed hard. "No, I haven't."

"It's fascinating," Anna continued. "The first thing she wrote was 'help me.' Can you imagine how exciting that must have been for her care givers, for her family?"

Samantha picked up the article and looked at the photo of the girl hugging her father. "It must have been amazing."

"She refused to sit down at the computer again for days, but the ABA trainers insisted that she attempt it again. They withheld reinforcers of course." Anna shook her head. "I have mixed feelings about their techniques."

"Yes, they have interesting techniques."

Anna looked up and raised a curious eyebrow at Samantha. Samantha licked her lips. She wasn't fooling Anna with her non-committal comments. Still she dipped her chin, saying nothing, feeling as if she and Anna were playing a round of poker. Anna blinked first. "At any rate," she said, "that's a completely different discussion. To the matter at hand." She pulled what appeared to be a ream of paper from the folder. "The online chatter has been voracious. I've been holding back, just watching. Some people think it's a fraud. Others are accusing the family of guiding her hand, the way facilitators did with autistic clients back in the early 90s. Were you aware of that movement? I've had my people doing research; it got a lot of play at the time. First as a phenomenon touting the intelligence of children and adults who seemingly had severe cognitive disabilities, and then the inevitable backlash, exposing facilitators as frauds. Most of them well meaning of course, but frauds nonetheless." She paused, flipping through the long columns of online discussion. "Do you remember all this from the 90s? I suppose you would have been a brand new teacher back then."

"I was aware of it, yes," Samantha said cautiously. She glared at the papers as Anna flipped through them, hoping she wouldn't ask anything else. Anna slid the papers back into the manila folder. A grouping of blue-inked pyramids had been drawn on the back of the folder. Samantha touched the edge of the folder before Anna could tuck it back into her purse. "What's with the pyramids?" she asked.

"Oh!" Anna looked a little embarrassed. "Just doodles. It actually helps me focus during long meetings."

Samantha nodded.

"I know that this is controversial territory," Anna said slowly, "but I am intrigued. I wasn't aware of facilitated communication back in its heyday. That was long before I adopted Luisa." She took a breath then spoke at a rapid clip. "I say nothing ventured, nothing gained. If I weren't a risk taker, I would never have opened my first pie shop in Berkeley years ago." She stared hard at Samantha. "Now my researchers say that facilitation is still being used as a viable therapy, but only if it can be faded out quickly so the client becomes an independent typist. This is still being done in upstate New York and a few other places around the world. It's being done quietly, so as not to expose families to ridicule." She beat her pen softly against the table as she spoke. "If I weren't so close to another shop opening, I'd just pull Luisa out of school and take her back to New York immediately. But I can't do that right now. So I'm asking you to help me out." She paused to look significantly at Samantha, but the teacher waited, her tongue pressed against her lips. Anna continued. "Would you be willing to give facilitated communication a try, Samantha? It could be an exciting adventure for all of us."

Samantha felt like she was being pressured to join a cult. She stared at the table, the silence throwing a heavy blanket onto her head. She wanted to claim ignorance of the method, but she couldn't do that. "Well, I guess it wouldn't hurt to try," Samantha said tentatively.

Anna grinned. "I knew you had an adventurous streak in you!" she exclaimed. "You'd have to, wouldn't you?—to take on such a challenging job to begin with."

Samantha smiled, but sidestepped the compliments. "You know, Anna, this is something you could do yourself at home. You really don't need my help," She paused to inject a self-deprecating tone in her voice. "Of course, I am happy to assist if I can, but you don't need a teaching credential to try this out."

"Agreed," Anna noted, returning to a business-like demeanor. "But I felt it would be more effective if we coordinated our efforts."

Samantha nodded, hoping she was able to hide her discomfort. "Of course."

"Now as I said, business commitments prevent me from traveling to New York until January, so I'm working on another plan."

She smiled smugly, quite pleased with herself. "This is a case of getting the mountain to come to Mohammed."

Samantha took a deep breath, feeling almost a little scared this time. "I'm working on getting one of those New York professors to come out here. And why wouldn't he? I could arrange a few side trips for him to his choice of beaches, anywhere on the west coast or Hawaii. And when I persuade him to leave his classes and come here, then we'll have a little seminar—you, me and Luisa's care givers—and I'm sure we'll come away with a wealth of information."

Samantha stared dumbfounded at the power of this woman. She suddenly realized that her mouth was open and she closed it.

Anna's eyes narrowed, perhaps sensing Samantha's surprise. "When I see what I want I create a plan and I go after it. My years in business have prepared me well for all facets of life." Her tone was insistent and unapologetic, though there was a note of defensiveness there as well.

Samantha shrugged. "I guess I was thinking that we could just try FC with Luisa. You know, like I said, it wouldn't hurt to just try."

Anna leaned forward with a mild smile. "Ms O'Malley, are you holding out on me?" she asked playfully. "I wouldn't know how to 'just try.' Perhaps you do? Have you done facilitated communication before—or as you say with your more familiar lingo—FC?"

Samantha felt herself blush. "Well, I uh, attended conferences when I was first teaching. It was a very interesting topic." She paused to collect her thoughts. "Look, why don't you give me the weekend to dig through old files and find my notes on it all. Maybe I'd be ready to try something next week. As you say, nothing ventured, nothing gained. If I have no success, then I'd certainly look forward to meeting with the experts. But this could save us some time, maybe."

Anna turned her head to gaze at Samantha from the corner of her eyes. "You most certainly may give it a go next week if you'd like," Anna conceded. She stood abruptly, slinging her large purse over her shoulder and extending a hand to Samantha. "I look forward to getting to know you better, Samantha. You're not showing me all your cards yet, and you know what? I like that. I respect that. I think we're still in the exploratory stage of our relationship, but you'll see that I can be a helpful partner in many ways. Eventually, we'll come to trust each other—and you know what—I want you to use me. I have many resources. Take advantage: I believe in public education and I want to be helpful. And I can be." She gave Samantha's hand a final shake. "I'll be in touch."

When I least expect it, Samantha thought as she watched Anna stride out the door. She sank back into her chair and buried her face in her hands. The door was still sliding closed when she heard it swing open again abruptly. Was Anna returning for an encore? She jerked her head up.

Charlie stood in the doorway. "Hey," he said in a low voice, as if afraid to speak louder. "You okay?"

She threw her shoulders back. "Yeah, I'm fine."

"Rough meeting?"

She crinkled her nose. "It was--" she searched for a word. "Different. The parents are different on this side of the river, Mystery." He sat across from her at the table and she smiled at him. "So what're you doing here on campus so late?"

He grinned. "I was hoping for more pie," he said.

"I put that pie in the staff room yesterday," she reminded him. "Nothing but crumbs by now."

"Well, as I recall, Ms Omm had other ways of providing me with dessert," he said suggestively.

"Get over yourself," she said playfully as she tossed a yellow marker in his direction, hitting him square in the chest.

He picked up the marker, but before he could toss it back, there was a rap at the front door. She got up and walked wearily across the room. It was Adam Yang with another box. "Strawberry cheesecake," he announced. "Ms Villaseñor thanks you for your time."

CHAPTER SEVEN

"What'd you get?" Samantha asked Charlie as she held her front door open for him.

"A surprise," he said insistently as he strode across the tiled entryway. "I hope you didn't set the table. This is picnic food."

"Oh, Charlie, why can't anything ever be simple?"

"Gee, Sam, most women love this whimsical romantic side I have."

"I just like to be fed when I'm hungry!" she said.

He leaned in to kiss her, and she let him. His lips tasted salty. He'd been eating something in the car. "French fries. Did you buy French fries?"

"Those are gone," he admitted. "But you'll love the rest. Where's that big old blanket we used to take with us to the river? Still in the trunk of your car?"

"I'll get it; it's in the linen closet off the guest bathroom."

"I'll get us a roll of paper towels from the kitchen. We don't need anything as formal as paper napkins, just paper to staunch the grease."

She got the blanket and they set up camp in the dirt of the atrium. "Hey you've done a little work out here," he said admiring. "I'm impressed. What's this—a dogwood and a rose of Sharon? Very nice."

"I'm just getting started," she said. "It'll be a long journey." She looked around the atrium, surveying her work proudly. Maybe the word *journey* would prove to be more than a metaphor. Maybe she could pour all her infertility frustrations into this space and create the most opulent, fragrant, and fertile refuge for birds and butterflies--as well as the broken-hearted and confused.

"Well," Charlie was saying, as he lifted food from greasy brown bags, "every journey begins with a single step."

She smiled at him. Charlie had always enjoyed gardening. He would help her if she asked. And why shouldn't she ask?

He offered her a burger. "Here you go: single patty for Ms Omm, double patty for Mystery, and loads of onion rings to share."

"Willie's onion rings!" she exclaimed as she scooped up one of the massive rings, bigger and fatter than any jelly donut. "I knew that's where you were going. Now remember, I have told you this before: we cannot make a habit of these. Way too much fat!"

"And why are you telling me this, Sam? Unless you're planning on making a habit out of me?"

She playfully waved an onion ring at him. "Eat your burger, Mystery."

"Give me some credit for remembering that you wouldn't want a soda to add to all these calories. See," he said, shaking the paper cup, "ice water."

"Very thoughtful of you, Mr. Easter." She inserted a straw through the plastic lid, and took a small sip.

"So did the Dragon Pie Lady upset your apple cart this afternoon?" he asked.

She paused with a mouthful of burger. "What do you mean?"

"You looked all shook up when I came in," he told her. "I figured she must have been making big time demands on you."

Samantha shrugged as she nibbled on an onion ring. "She certainly has some original ideas."

Charlie raised an eyebrow. "Not your typical requests for

applied behavior consultants and one-on-one assistants to hold the kid's hand all day?"

Samantha rolled her eyes. Many savvy parents these days were asking for one-on-one aides to assist their children during each school day. An expensive proposition for cash-strapped school districts, but was it worth it? Samantha refused to weigh in on the question, since she'd had no experience with such requests in her career in the larger inner-city district. She swallowed a bite of hamburger and shook her head at Charlie. "She hasn't asked for that yet. The minute she requests more personnel I will direct her to the admins at the district office. I'm not going to go ten rounds with her. I'd lose in a bout with that woman. She is too polished."

Charlie reached for an onion ring. "So what does she want?"

"Oh, gosh," Samantha said hoping to change the subject. "It's just a crazy notion she's got. I can go along for a while I guess; we'll just have to see." She looked over at Charlie. "You want some catsup for the onion rings? I can get some in the kitchen."

"No, you're the catsup queen, Sam; I don't need any." He swallowed a mouthful. "You want me to get you some?"

"No, I'm fine."

"You just don't want to talk about Mrs. Strawberry Cheesecake. I get it. I don't know why. I mean you got your sensitive man here, your primo listener, and you never want to talk anymore. You used to be quite the raconteur, Ms Omm, regaling friend and foe with merry tales. Now you're oh-so-tight lipped."

"That's not true," she said, pushing away an onion ring.

He gave a half frown and a shrug. "Whatever. We can talk about movies or novels or TV shows if you prefer."

She gave his shoulder a little slap, but still she said nothing. He grinned and looked at her. "What?" he asked.

"Nothing, Charlie," she said. "You're just—you know—so easy to be with. I like being here with you."

He put his arm around her. "I like being here with you too,

Sam."

He leaned in and she opened her mouth to allow his tongue to play around her lips. "Chilies on the burger, huh?" she asked.

He laughed. "Yeah."

"Interesting choice." She kissed him again. "Next time I'd appreciate it if you'd just go for the extra pickle."

His hand slid down toward her ribs, but she pushed him away. "We haven't even had dessert yet, Charlie," she admonished him. "Remember we've got a very large cheesecake to take care of."

He laughed. "I've got something extra large to take care of too," he told her. "I think I'll need a second helping of sugar."

He tipped her back onto the blanket as she hastily cleared a space between cups of water, catsup packets and a few left over onion rings. "How many times have we made love on this blanket, O'Malley?" he asked her.

She giggled. "You can get nostalgic later, Mystery. I need some of those tasty kisses now."

He kissed her mouth and her throat and then pulled her blouse up to kiss her breasts. She closed her eyes and thought of nothing but his lips, and how good it felt to be with him, no one else but him. As he headed south, he paused before unzipping her pants. "So," he whispered, "where are you in your cycle?"

She half sat up. "Doesn't matter, remember? I don't have to worry about that anymore."

"I'm sorry; I forgot."

She lay back down on her side and he spooned around her. "It's okay. It's a process, you know, the doctors tell me that. It's a grieving process, and it's okay. It's O-kay." She turned to face him. "Maybe that's why you're here, to help me with the grieving. Have a little fun, help me realize life goes on."

"Happy to help," he said, pressing his smile up against her mouth. She gave him a quick peck, then wrapped her arms around his neck. She pulled him tight against her chest so he wouldn't see her blinking back tears.

***

Later they showered, pulled on terrycloth robes and hunkered down on the couch to share the enormous cheesecake. "Thank God it's Friday. This much indulgence for one night will not make a happy morning." Samantha sighed as she slid a forkful of creamy goodness between her teeth. "Ooo—these strawberries are amazing! So sweet."

"Not bad," he agreed, "though I think it's a little heavy on the vanilla."

She made a face at him. "Is your palate really that refined? I can't pick out vanilla."

"Of course my palate is that refined, Sam. That's why I'm drawn to you. You taste better than any woman I've ever known."

She looked at him in shock. "I've never thought of that before," she admitted. "But you taste pretty good too."

"See," he gloated. "There are no coincidences! That means something."

They each took another bite, and she held the pie in her mouth running her tongue through it slowly with an appraising aim. "Nope, can't find the vanilla."

He laughed. "Don't worry about it. Just enjoy it."

She smiled as they each took another bite. "This woman will make me fat if she keeps up this pie ritual after every meeting."

"So you expect the meetings to continue?"

"Oh, I don't know what's going to happen, Charlie. She may zip out of here as fast as she arrived. She's on a fast track."

"Hmmm," he mused still eating. "Enjoy it while it lasts."

She swallowed and held up her fork as if reaching a milestone.

"She wants me to try facilitated communication with her daughter."

"What's that?"

"You've heard of it. It was all the rage back in the early 90s."

"I was a new Dad in the early 90s, trying to come to term with the fact that I shouldn't tear out of town whenever the notion struck me now that I had a son." He took a last bite and pushed the cheesecake away. "I wasn't interested in whatever was the latest rage."

Samantha stared down at the pie plate for a moment, suddenly lost in the notion that things might have been different if she had met Charlie when they were younger, before he'd become a father. Might they have conceived a baby together back then? How different her life would have been if Dale had been *her* son.

He squeezed her knee and brought her out of her musing. "Something tells me this facilitated communication was a big piece of your decade back then."

"That something that told you about it was me, silly! I told you all about it, back when we first met. It was something important that happened to--" she stopped abruptly.

"What?"

"I don't know! That's just it—I don't know!" She stretched her legs out toward him and he lifted her feet into his lap. "I was about to say that it was something that happened *to me.* But that's not right. I don't know what is right. Maybe it was something that I *made* happen. Maybe it was something that I *needed* to make happen. Maybe I just wanted some sort of confirmation that I was in the right place. But instead I was left confused and disappointed and depressed. In other words, highly susceptible to the charms of one Charles Allen Easter."

He smirked, playing along in a whimsical tone. "That's my style, all right, to swoop in when a woman is vulnerable after some kind of personal or professional downfall, and pick up the pieces real fast for her, before she realizes what's happening. Then I swoop out. I only stuck around with you because you taste so good, Sam."

She snorted a short laugh.

"So, uh, I've forgotten what facilitated communication is," he admitted. " Tell me about it."

"I thought you were a good listener!" she said, feigning disappointment.

"Mea culpa," he pleaded.

She shrugged to signal her forgiveness, then launched in. "Well, it was a technique developed—or discovered—or something—first by a woman in Australia, then some professors at the University of Syracuse in New York picked up on it, and really started to run with it. It got loads of publicity."

"What kind of a technique was it?"

"Well, essentially, it's a way to help a person with autism or another cognitive disability communicate with the world. You take their hand, just to steady it, not to guide them, and then they can type. And suddenly we were learning that they were a lot more intelligent than we'd ever known before."

Charlie stared at her. "You told me about doing this? Why don't I remember?"

"I guess I didn't tell you a lot of details. I wanted to tell you—I wanted to share it with someone—but I was embarrassed. I felt like such a failure!"

He stared at her intently. "Tell me more," he urged, giving her foot a squeeze.

She nodded, settling back against some pillows. "It was my first year teaching. It was not going well. I was overwhelmed with the kids, and the paperwork and the demands of a very negative principal! The staff used to call her 'the rampaging bitch.'"

Charlie smiled, but allowed her to continue.

"Then I met Craig."

"Oh, I do remember you talking about Craig," he said. "He was one of the school's custodians, wasn't he?"

"That's right. He was the substitute night custodian. He showed up sometime around February and he stayed till June. I wonder if I'd still be a teacher if it weren't for Craig. He really pulled me through that first year."

CHAPTER EIGHT

Craig reminded Samantha of a large puppy, galumphing after her through the school. He was tall, at least 6'3". Despite being well into his thirties, his slender arms and legs made him seem as gangly as a teenager. He was relentlessly cheerful with an infectious smile so broad it sent laugh lines fanning across his cheeks and jaw. Nonetheless, Samantha didn't want to be bothered. She was not happy on this campus, and she was none too pleased that this lanky stranger had shown up midterm to hit on her.

He'd appear in her room minutes after the kids had left, interrupting any moments of silence and solitude she could muster after a long day with boisterous children. He'd lug his vacuum cleaner up into her inconvenient trailer, and then he'd start a steady stream of banal chatter. Earnest observations on the weather, on school climate, on lack of parental responsibility. She felt herself an unskilled conversationalist, nodding, yet reluctant to agree, lest he find her attractive and want to stick around. Most days she'd stuff her tote bag full of papers and books, beat a hasty retreat to her second hand VW rabbit, and hit the asphalt heading home, somewhat resentful that he had chased her from her classroom.

One day in April her classroom was burglarized. The thieves had taken a computer, a vacuum cleaner, a camera, and a boxful of children's board games. When she discovered the robbery in the morning, she had rushed to the office to report it to the principal. A cluster of male teachers and custodians was gathered around the front desk, berating the Kings' coach for the basketball team's latest loss. Samantha wiggled through to make eye contact with the square-jawed old secretary. Her name was Veronica, Ronnie for short. "Someone broke into my classroom!" Samantha exclaimed.

Ronnie's mouth puckered as if she'd been eating dill pickles. "So what do you want me to do about it?" she spat.

Samantha felt slapped. "Won't you call the police?" she asked meekly.

"What good would that do?" Ronnie asked. "This kind of thing happens all the time around here."

Fred, the head custodian nodded, pulling his black glasses from his face to emphasize his point. "Especially this time of year," he said pointing his specs at her. "The thieves come out in the spring; be grateful it's nearly summer."

Samantha trudged dejected back to her hovel of a room, ten minutes before her students were to arrive, nearly reduced to tears. It was a very long day.

After putting the students on the buses at three, Samantha stopped in the office to call her insurance agent to see if her renter's insurance would pay for any of the lost property. Nope. Well, she should have seen that coming.

When she got back to the trailer, the doors were locked and she had forgotten her key inside on her desk. Great. The end to another perfect day. But wait—she could hear something inside—the roar of the vacuum cleaner. Craig must still be there. She banged on the door. Nothin'. She banged some more. Still nothin'! Finally she kicked the door. Bobbie, the chinless teacher across the way, stuck her pointy nose out to glare at Samantha. If anybody had a stick up her butt it was Bobbie. Samantha had rarely met anyone so self-righteous. She opened her mouth to explain her situation to Bobbie, but then she closed it. Why bother? She turned her back to Bobbie and gave one final sharp rap. The door at the other end of the trailer opened and Craig stuck his head out. They gaped at each other in surprise for a moment, as if they were two people from a different planet who had each traveled separately to earth. Well, fancy meeting you here.

"I'll be right there," Craig said, closing his door. She waited quietly pointing her nose toward the door, feeling Bobbie's glare burning the back of her neck. Craig opened the door with a grin and swung it open as if she were a trick or treater that he was amazed to see at his home. He gave a friendly but curt nod to Bobbie in the hallway below. "Mrs. Jones." He closed the door. "She's a nice lady," he said, "but she sure is nosy."

Samantha turned to look at him abruptly. She'd never heard him make a disparaging remark about anyone. She gave him a quizzical look.

"You need to watch your back sometimes," he told her with a knowing nod.

Samantha felt a jolt of adrenaline. "What do you mean? Have you heard people gossip about me?"

"Oh, no, nothing like that. I'm just speaking globally—you know."

She gazed at him for a moment. Most days she would have hastened to her desk to start filling up her tote bag to make a quick get-away. But for some reason, she was lingering. She didn't even want to stay; she just couldn't get herself to move any faster. "Oh," she said, her voice sounding frailer than she'd like to admit.

She wandered to her desk and sat down at the uncomfortable district-issue straight-backed chair. He leaned against the doorjamb a few feet away. "I heard about the burglary in here," he said gently. "That must have been pretty upsetting."

She looked up at him in surprise. At her break she'd left voice mail messages for her principal, her program specialist and the director of the special ed department. No one had responded. This was the first time anyone had mentioned the incident all day. This was the first word of kindness. She blinked rapidly. "I'm so tired," she blurted without thinking.

"Well, it was an emotional shock for you to come in and see how your room had been violated. That will tire you out. You should take extra care of yourself tonight. Have a glass a wine, or some ice cream." He stared into the distance, then smiled and turned to her. "You really like ice cream, don't you? Especially chocolate."

Samantha pulled her head back. "Why do you say that? I mean, how do you know--"

"I'm just reading the energy, Samantha, that's all."

She stared at him, feeling a little spooked, but she didn't move. She stared down at her hands. "You know what? You're the first person all day who's offered me any sympathy that my classroom was burglarized. Everybody else seems to think it's no big deal." She coughed, afraid she would tear up. "This is such an unfriendly place," she concluded in a near whisper, then she looked up at him. "Don't you think this is an unfriendly place?"

He smiled mildly and shook his head. "No, that's not it. I mean there's the same kind of push and pull you get anywhere there's a group of diverse people brought in and forced to work together. That's typical. Your problem is that you're so much more spiritually advanced than anybody else here, you can't relate to them—and vice versa."

Samantha resisted a temptation to roll her eyes. She called it the special ed aura: an assumption that she was kinder, stronger, more patient, able to withstand more abuse, and endure it more cheerfully than your average everyday woman. If he told her she was going to get a crown in heaven, she just might hurl. She took a deep breath. "You know," she said, a fair amount of sarcasm in her tone, "just because I'm a special education teacher doesn't mean I'm a saint."

He burst out laughing. "That's so funny," he said. "I didn't say you were a saint! Far from it! It doesn't have anything to do with you being a special education teacher. You'd be special no matter what you did, even if you worked in a closet shuffling papers and never saw anybody else all day. You'd still be special."

She was dumbfounded by his unexpected praise. "What are you talking about?" she finally managed.

"You're an advanced soul! You know this is true, so don't look so shocked."

She smiled self-consciously, pleased he was trying to flatter her but annoyed at herself for caring. "I don't get it," she said. "You don't know me. But you seem to know I'm interested in—well, what would you call it—spirituality? God? That's not the kind of thing people can tell just by looking at you."

"I can."

She stood to retrieve her tote bag from a nearby cabinet, frustrated that he wasn't more forthcoming with an explanation. She was intrigued, but she didn't want to admit it. "And just how can you tell—uh, someone's level of spirituality? Is it my clothes, my shoes, the color of my hair?"

He laughed. "No, no. Samantha, it's all vibrations. I can tell by your vibrations."

She glared at him, then sat again at her desk. "Vibrations," she repeated, giving him her teacher stare, waiting for him to elaborate.

"Exactly!" he exclaimed, taking a step toward the desk, gesturing deliberately with outstretched fingers. "Everybody vibrates. At the cellular level. At the atomic level. Remember your basic physics. That's how it works, everything vibrates. And the faster you vibrate, the higher your level of spiritual awareness."

"But we can't see these vibrations."

"Not with our eyes, no," he admitted. "But I sense it. Intuitively. I just know."

She thought it sounded crazy, but it also made her feel smug. "And I vibrate faster than everybody else here?"

He smiled. "You vibrate faster than everybody else here—except for me."

She laughed, dismissively, wanting to appear aloof. "But of course."

He nodded, still smiling, though she sensed he knew she was skeptical. "There are seven planes of spirituality. I have reached the apex. I'm at the seventh plane."

"Okay. So where am I?"

He squinted as if taking a closer peek. "I'd say high second, low third."

She scowled. "That's not so high."

He leaned toward her. "You have to understand that very few

advanced souls have chosen to incarnate at this point in time. Most people on earth aren't on the planes at all."

She leaned back in her chair, suddenly realizing that she wanted to believe it, she wanted to believe herself special. He continued.

"You've always known you were different, Samantha. You've always known that you were special. People have tried to tell you, but you just didn't believe them. That's why I'm here now. You knew you'd be having trouble about now, you knew you would need help. That's why you chose to have me come to you. This is not subtle. You. Are. Special."

***

"Did you and Craig become lovers?" Charlie asked.

Samantha looked into his eyes, liking the tiny bit of vulnerability she imagined there. "No," she answered quickly, giving his hand a squeeze. "It wasn't like that. It was just that Craig talked to me in a way no one else ever had."

"I've always told you you were special," Charlie said defensively.

She gave him a gentle kick. "Yeah, you say I taste better than any other woman. Now that's something I can put on a resume."

He grabbed her foot so she couldn't kick him again. "So what's Craig got to do with this facilitated communication?" Charlie asked.

Samantha looked down, feeling a little embarrassed. "Craig told me I had a special job to do during this incarnation. Something I had volunteered for."

"What was it?"

"He said I would know it because it would feel right, so I assumed I was there already: teaching my students who have disabilities." She shrugged. "But he said no, there would be something else. He didn't know what it was, but he said I'd know when the time was right."

"So," Charlie asked, "facilitated communication?"

Samantha nodded.

CHAPTER NINE

During her second year of teaching, Samantha went to a conference that included a session on facilitated communication. She thought it would be something about picture communication systems for nonverbal students. But the reality was much stranger. People from all over the country—New York, Florida, Michigan and Oregon—had come to testify to the truth of their experiences with students who had autism, severe cognitive disabilities and aphasia. From their different vantage points they were all having amazing sessions as these children revealed themselves to be intelligent and sensitive individuals. Samantha could hardly wait to get back to her classroom to try it out.

She tried the technique first with the most handicapped of her students. She got nowhere. The child sat in front of the typewriter rocking and moaning. She tried it with another of her autistic students. This boy proved sensitive to touch, and he backhanded her across the mouth when she tried to take his hand. She retreated back to the group where her aides oversaw the other children who sat quietly at desks writing their names and addresses. She strolled around the room, peeking over shoulders to see that progress was being made.

The room was quiet, and Samantha went to perch on a stool in the back to watch the proceedings. She heard a sound she hadn't noticed before: it was Jimmy, rocking gently and stimming—or stimulating himself--on his own monotonous nasal whine. Jimmy had Down's syndrome, so it had never occurred to her before that he might be on the autism spectrum as well. And yet here he was exhibiting some of the most classic symptoms. She stood up. "Jimmy," she said. "Come on back here and talk to me."

She led him to the back table and seated him by her old corona typewriter. "Hold on," she said. "Let me get this paper in here." She scrolled in a piece of typing paper on which she'd already typed several questions. She took his hand in hers, and gently folded back his fingers, leaving his index finger free to hunt for letters on the keyboard. "Now, I'm going to help you type, okay? But you have to do all the thinking. I'm not going to do it for you; I'm just going to steady your hand."

"Okay," the boy said in his low voice.

"Okay!" she agreed enthusiastically. "Here's the first question. Do you like ice cream? Now you type yes or no."

She held his hand tight as he reached for the keyboard. She pulled back as she'd been instructed to do, and he fought with her to reach the letter Y. He hit the Y. She took a deep breath and he leaned forward, reaching for the E. She held him back, pulling him away from the keyboard, but he pushed forward. He hit the E. Again she pulled back and he reached for the S. He did it. He had typed the word "YES." She'd had no idea he knew how to spell yes.

"Good, Jimmy," she praised him. "Now let's try this question: do you like broccoli?"

Again he typed YES. "You like broccoli?" she asked him again.

"Uh huh."

"That's amazing; I didn't know that."

They went through a series of questions: do you like TV shows, do you like books, do you like loud noises—and he answered YES, YES, and NO.

"What's your favorite lunch?" she read the next question.

PZZA, he typed. She held her breath. "Pizza," she said aloud. "What do you like on your pizza?" she asked, then realized that she was really pressing her luck. "You don't have to tell me if you don't want to," she said quickly, but his hand was already reaching for the keys. He hit the X and leaned on it hard. XXXXXXXXXXXX he typed.

She pulled his hand back. "Focus," she cautioned, leaning her elbow on the table to give her leverage. "Okay, ready when you are." He pushed forward again.

"OOOOOOOOOOOOPPPINNNNNNEAPPPPPPPPPPLLLLLLLLLE," he typed. She leaned back and stared at the page. "Did you say pineapple?" she asked.

"Uh huh."

"Pineapple," she repeated in disbelief. "Pineapple!" She grabbed the boy by the shoulders and gave him an impetuous hug. "Pineapple!" A bell rang and she looked at the clock. "Oh, gee it's time for recess. Look, let's just type your name, then we'll be done. Okay?" He quickly grabbed her hand, and forged ahead. "JIM," he typed.

"You're not done," she prompted.

He stared at her with sad eyes for a moment and then pushed forward again.

"IIIIIWANTTTTTTTTTTTTTTOOOOOOOOOOOBEEELIKE MYDAD." She stared at the long line of letters and her mouth dropped open.

"Okay; Jim it is. From now on I'll call you Jim." He laughed gleefully. "I'm so proud of you," she whispered.

***

Samantha spent the rest of the day typing with the children, and every one of them could do it. Her arms and shoulders ached when she put them on the bus. "I felt so happy at the end of that day," Samantha told Charlie. "I don't think I had ever been so happy."

"And what did Craig say when the facilitation was going so well?"

"Well, he was no longer working at the school by then. But coincidentally--"

"Hey, there's no such things as a coincidence, Samantha!"

"Right, not coincidently, but synchronistically, Craig called me that very night—the night after the day I'm managed to type with all the kids. I hadn't heard from him in weeks. I was so surprised—or actually not, not surprised at all. I mean it just made sense he would call."

"What did he say?"

"When I told him about how I'd discovered that all the kids could communicate through facilitation—well, I was essentially saying, 'Guess what! Every one of my developmentally disabled students—all these children that we thought couldn't read or write or do math—every last one of them—they're intelligent, they're witty, they're smart as little whips! They're in there! They're trapped in there, in their bodies, and they want to find a way out, and they have! We're finding that way together.' Oh, I was so excited. And he said very solemnly, 'This is it.' And I said, 'What are you talking about? This is what?'" She paused to take a breath. "He said, 'This is the special job you're meant to do.'"

"What a great validation!"

"Yes, but Charlie, like I said to Craig: how can that be? I didn't invent this. I didn't discover this. Other people around the world have been doing this for years. This is not something I came up with."

"He said, 'Samantha, it's true you didn't come up with this on your own, but you will be the focal point for the energy.' He said, 'Your vehicle,'—meaning my body—he told me my vehicle would serve as the matrix that would conduct this energy all over the world. He said, 'The energy will come from the Divine Source through you, and out to the earth plane.' That's what he told me. That's what he said would happen."

"Pretty heady stuff," Charlie noted.

"Yeah, but I bit right into it. I was so anxious for approval."

"Sam," Charlie said thoughtfully, "are you telling me you wouldn't buy this now? If Craig showed up and told you this same story today, you'd say 'No, thanks, I don't believe this, this is crazy?'"

She stared at him on the other end of the couch, still holding her foot, and she wondered if maybe she wouldn't like another bite of the cheesecake. If she wouldn't like to make love again. If she wouldn't like to retreat to a cozy and sweet physical sensation and forget that this wild tale was part of her past, that it had all really happened to her.

"No," she admitted. "You got me. I wouldn't trade this experience for all the sanity in the world."

He threw his arms in the air enthusiastically. "Of course you wouldn't! Samantha! You've told me bits and pieces about this before, but never with so much detail! This was important to you, wasn't it? And yet, here you are, talking tentatively as if you're ashamed of it. You were involved in something amazing. Why don't you embrace it?"

"But Charlie," she pleaded, "it all went south. First the media embraced us: we were fantastic and outrageous and joyful! Then we were frauds! We were guiding their hands, we were making it all up, we were deceiving desperate families who were so hungry for a little scrap of hope. Some of us, they said, were dupes ourselves. We were well meaning, but we were delusional. Others of us were flat out charlatans. We should be dismissed from our jobs, or even locked up, for taking advantage of the families of children with severe disabilities. How shameful we were. It was unforgiveable."

"But Samantha!" he exclaimed. "You knew the truth. You knew it was genuine. Why worry?"

She studied her fingernails and pursed her lips. "I don't know," she said finally.

"Well you had to know it was genuine, didn't you?"

Samantha shrugged. "It's been twelve years now. I can remember how I felt at the time: I know I felt confident that I was doing the right thing back then. But when I think of it now, it's like I'm watching someone else, an actress in a play. Was that really me? Did that really happen? It's surreal."

Charlie lowered his eyebrows and bent toward her. "I don't understand. You knew you weren't guiding their hands, right?"

She took a deep breath. "Sometimes," she said slowly, "I wondered if maybe I was guiding their hands. I didn't mean to. I didn't think I was. I tried looking away, but it was so much easier when I was watching them type, you know, following the conversation. Sometimes it just felt as if we were creating something together."

"I could understand how that could be possible," Charlie said.

She looked up at him and they shared a long meaningful gaze. His tone had been reassuring, and yet she could sense the doubt in his voice. "It's okay," she said. "I'm not sure I believe it either."

"I didn't say I didn't believe it, Sam." He paused, taking a deep breath, as if weighing his words carefully. "What's important is what you believe. You say you were confident and sure of the validity back then—well, you were right in the middle of it then—the way you were feeling back then was accurate. It was true and you knew it. Since then you've had a lot of years to grow doubtful, to create an alternative version of what happened, based primarily on your concerns of what other people think."

She nodded rapidly. "I know, Charlie, you're right."

"Listen," he said, "Close your eyes." She gave him a look of curiosity masked with annoyance, but he persisted. "C'mon, close your eyes for a minute." She complied and he spoke in a soft rhythmic voice. "Take yourself back to that day you facilitated the first time with Jimmy. Remember the rush you felt as his hand glided across the keyboard. Remember that!"

She opened her eyes quickly. "Charlie! You know what the amazing thing was?"

"What?"

"Everything. That year, everything was amazing." She paused to look at him. "My students were eager to type with me. They all wanted a turn. They'd give up recess to type with me. Of course I had no doubts." She leaned forward. "But even outside the classroom when I was out with friends, or at home, or in the grocery store, I knew things. I knew what people were going to say before they said it; I knew what was going to happen. When I drove to my favorite coffee house on 21st Street, a parking spot would immediately become available right in front of the door. When I'd go to my favorite Mexican restaurant, even on a Saturday night, a table would open up just as I walked in. I'd think of someone I wanted to see, and they'd call me. It was outrageous. It was like I was riding a wave. It was like being in one of those big airports with the moving sidewalks and you can stride along the conveyor belt and feel like you're some kind of Olympic marathon runner, and you've just hit the wall, and you've got this big burst of energy and it's carrying you through a crack that opens up in the mob of people jogging along beside you, but you just surge forward and leave them all in the dust! I felt like I was in a dream—that I was dreaming all the time, and in all the dreams I was flying!"

Charlie laughed. "That's how you should feel all the time, Sam! That's what it's like to be awake and to know you're in the right place!"

She looked at him skeptically. "Are you telling me you feel that way all the time?"

He gave a curt nod. "A lot of the time, yeah. Not all the time."

She shrugged. "I don't know how you can maintain a feeling like that, Charlie. I mean it'd be like having an orgasm for a week. It'd be exhausting."

Charlie laughed. "I think I could handle that kind of exhaustion."

She playfully slapped his knee. "Oh, get over yourself, Mystery."

"Okay, Sam, you're right; I know we've both got a ways to go before either one of us reaches enlightenment. But don't you see: what you experienced a dozen years ago was genuine. You knew it then, and you can't let fading memories and belligerent critics take that away from you."

"Yeah, I guess," she said in a soft voice.

"'I guess,'" he mocked her in a teasing tone. "C'mon Sam. I'm not asking you to vote for Hitler; I'm asking you to believe in yourself— and in your own experience, your own knowledge."

"Charlie, you just don't know how painful it was back then."

"Why, Sam? Because a few know-nothing critics wrote articles and produced insulting TV stories? You didn't stop facilitating with the kids because of a little negative press, did you?"

"What if I did, Charlie? You weren't there; you don't know. Would you judge me?"

He looked surprised; his voice went low. "No, I'm sorry," he said. "I wouldn't judge you, Sam. You're right: I wasn't there, and I don't know. But I will say this: I don't believe it. Something else must have happened—pressure from administrators, threats to dismiss you—I can't believe Samantha O'Malley just up and quit."

She shook her head. "Maybe Samantha O'Malley got burnt out. It happens, Charlie, and I shouldn't have to feel ashamed of that."

He shrugged but said nothing.

She stared at her hands for a moment. "But you're right. I didn't quit. The kids quit. They just stopped. I'd go to type with them, and they'd type gibberish. Or they'd type the same word over and over again. It was crazy, and there didn't seem to be anything I could do about it."

"What word would they type?"

She glanced up in surprise at the question. "Oh, I don't know," she said quickly, feeling embarrassed. "I don't really remember. Different kids would type different things."

"That's really strange."

"There'd been so much negative criticism in the media. I was scared. I couldn't help it," she admitted "I tried over and over again to type with the kids without watching our hands, just letting them go wherever they could without me knowing where they were going." She smiled. "One time, I put math worksheets in the typewriter. Just simple addition problems—two one-digit numbers. Like 2 plus 3. And I held each kid's hand really really tight, and then I looked away—up at the ceiling or off in the distance. I was determined to see if they could do this without my help—at least not my knowledgeable help—you know what I mean."

He nodded. "Yeah."

"I started with Jim; he was so easy going, I liked to try things out with him first. So I've got the worksheet in there and I'm holding Jim's hand really tight. I said to him, 'Two plus three: type the answer!' Then I looked away. I was pulling his hand back like crazy, trying to make it hard for him. I could sense that he was moving down away from the numbers into the letters, and I thought, gosh darn it!—he can't do it. He doesn't even understand that this is a math problem. He's just going to type some gibberish since I'm not watching and I can't guide his hand. But I still pulled back, even trying a little bit to direct higher—toward where I thought the row of numbers was, but no, he was determined to hit something, he knew where he wanted to go—and then finally he made contact—he hit a key, and I looked up and I saw two plus three equals five! He'd hit the five! I was astounded. I nearly cried. And then we went on, and we did four more math problems, just those easy ones, four plus three, six plus two—easy stuff, but easy stuff that disabled students usually couldn't do. And yet, with me holding his hand, not looking, staring at the ceiling—Jim was able to type the correct answer to four more problems. I was ecstatic. But you know what—those five problems took us forty minutes to complete. Forty minutes of physical struggle. So maybe he knew a few math facts, maybe it was a fluke--"

"It wasn't a fluke, Sam!" Charlie interjected.

"I know; I've always known. But forty minutes to test one kid. And what did I prove—nothing! Absolutely nothing. What did he learn doing that? I didn't teach him any new mathematical concepts doing that. I couldn't teach like that. I didn't know what to do. So when they stopped typing with me, I was disappointed. Hell, I was devastated for a while. But it was kind of a relief. What can I say? It was just so hard, Charlie. I was so confused."

"Sam, you just have to accept that you did the best you could with the knowledge that you had."

Samantha stared at her fingers. "When I think about it all now," she said, "I wonder if Craig duped me. I was lonely, I was insecure, and he was feeding my ego."

"No, Samantha," Charlie reassured her. "Believing the things Craig told you about yourself doesn't feed your ego. Not believing what he told you is what would feed your ego."

She shook her head. "I don't get it."

He gave her a curt nod. "Listen: it's the resistance in weight-bearing exercises that makes our muscles stronger. And it's resistance to truth that makes our egos stronger. Craig was telling you the truth: you are special, you are an advanced spiritual being. I know that. You just need to know it yourself."

At the moment she wanted to tell Charlie she loved him, but she held her breath. She couldn't throw her heart out on her sleeve, not this time. She leaned back with a sigh and stared at the ceiling.

He squeezed her foot. "Now the pie lady wants to give Ms Omm another go at facilitated communication," he said. "Maybe this is your big chance."

"My big chance?" She held her breath for a moment. Was the universe handing her another assignment? She wasn't sure how she'd feel about that.

"Hey, embrace this opportunity, Sam. Maybe this is what you've been waiting for."

"I'm scared, Charlie! Don't you get it? When I think back at all that, I feel like I must have fallen down the rabbit hole—and sometimes I'm still trying to find my way back up to the surface. This is scary territory for me!"

He shifted positions on the couch to wrap his arms around her shoulders. "So let's not think about it anymore tonight. Tomorrow's Saturday. And hey, Monday's Labor Day. So you've got three days to let this go. Let's go to bed."

CHAPTER TEN

Samantha strolled across a grassy plain, a warm breeze feathering through her hair. She seemed to be walking in high-heeled stilettos, something she never wore even with her dressiest outfits. They made her so tall her antenna brushed against the eucalyptus leaves. Wow, those smelled good. She tipped her head back and took a low-lying leaf into her mouth. It was fragrant and crisp against her long tongue, so flavorful. A rush of sensation flooded her nostrils, her eyes watered. But still she was distracted by these high-heels. She glanced down. Her legs were long and thin, but quite shapely, and very attractive if she did say so herself. They were spotted with a very pretty yellow and brown. Oh, that explains it, Samantha thought. I'm a giraffe. I'm a giraffe, and I'm on the savannah, and these crisp green leaves are absolutely delectable.

At her right ear a squawk and a chatter prompted her to rear her head back in surprised annoyance. She turned to see a yellow-billed magpie hovering at her very high eye level. She didn't know what the bird was saying, but she knew he was beckoning her. He flitted off, but could she follow? Wouldn't she have to proceed slowly with these stilt-like legs? She started tentatively but soon discovered she could move though space like a rocket. Her large body was perfectly designed for speed, her long legs carrying her through the sky as if she were a bird. She was exhilarated, racing at the magpie's side, filled with joy at this new adventure. The bird was happy too: she could sense it! She was laughing and he was pleased to have brought her here to this place, this pocket of satisfaction, this amazing universe.

***

She felt Charlie pressing up against her back, reaching his arm around her waist to spoon with her. She took his hand in hers, brought it to her lips and kissed his palm. "Morning," she said, rolling around to face him.

"Morning," he responded, then kissed her mouth lightly.

"I had the weirdest dream," she told him. "Well, actually, it's just the latest in a series of weird dreams."

"A series, huh?" Charlie asked. "Are they suitable for family TV or are they going to be comic books?"

"I don't know," she said with a giggle. "Maybe they'll be National Geographic specials!"

"Dare I ask: are your dreams breaking new frontiers in the field of science or medicine?"

"Don't be silly!" she said. "I'm just dreaming that I'm an animal."

"Well, I can attest to that; you are definitely an animal!" He growled suggestively and gave her another quick kiss, rubbing his unshaven cheek against her neck.

She pushed him back. "Cut it out, that tickles."

"So what kind of animal do you fancy yourself in these dreams?" he asked. "No, let me guess—you're a cat, right?"

"Too obvious, Mystery," she said smugly. "Though you're close. Once I dreamed I was a jaguar."

"Wow," he mused. "Classy and sexy. I like it."

"I've also dreamt I was a polar bear."

"Yeah, polar bears." He shook his head. "Not so sexy. Living on the tundra, they need a lot of fat packed onto their haunches to keep themselves warm. I hate to seem shallow, but I find it hard to get interested in a woman with that much bulk, Sam. So please stick to the feline family in your fantasies, okay?"

She gave him a playful slap on his shoulder. "I'm not the one with the weird fantasies, Mystery. This is just my subconscious going wild on me." She paused. "Last night I was a giraffe."

"Okay, that's just weird," he said laughing. "So you were like one of those Amazonian super model types with legs that go up to their chins—is that what you're talking about?"

She laughed hysterically. "I am talking about no such thing! I'm talking about a giraffe. Just an ordinary giraffe, strolling over your run of the mill grassy plain in Africa, minding her own business, not trying to live up to the bizarre expectations of Charlie Easter, just being a giraffe."

They both leaned back in the bed, literally rolling in laughter. "Very weird. Just a giraffe."

"That's right. Just a giraffe, talking to a yellow-billed magpie."

Charlie sat up and stared down at her. "A magpie? The giraffe was talking to a yellow-billed magpie?"

She rose up to confront him eye to eye. "That's right, a magpie," she declared. "You got a problem with that, Easter? You think a giraffe shouldn't be engaging in interspecies socialization? You think it's not right for giraffes and magpies to be friends? Is that what you think?"

Charlie swung his legs out of bed and reached for his pants. "Hey, I'm a big believer in freedom of association. If a giraffe and a yellow-billed magpie want to hang out together, if they want to date, or even stand before family, friends and God and declare their intentions to be truly joined spouses till death do them part—hey, it's fine with me. I say live and let live. I think it's not likely, but if it were to come to pass, I certainly wouldn't object."

"Not likely you say," Samantha said, continuing down this silly metaphorical road. "Well who are you to judge, Charlie? I know, anatomically speaking, that a giraffe and a magpie may have some issues with mating, but true love conquers all!"

"Anatomy, sure," Charlie agreed as he zipped his fly, "that would be a challenge. But so would geography. I mean those two species don't exactly hang out in the same environs you know."

"No, I guess not," Samantha conceded.

"You realize, don't you, Sam, that the yellow-billed magpie only lives here."

She bowed her head and pointed down at the bed. "Here?"

He spread his arms, circling his outstretched hands. "Here! In the central valley of California. Really. Birders come from all over the world to get a glimpse of them. Here. This is the only place."

"Really? I didn't know that!"

"Yeah, and good luck to them," Charlie said as he buttoned his shirt. "I haven't seen one in years. West Nile Virus may have wiped them out."

"No!"

"It's true," he said, sitting back down to stroke her shoulder. "I've heard they may be coming back, but I haven't seen them in a good long while."

"Used to be all over my parents' back yard near the river when I was growing up," she said.

"Yeah, I know." He smiled. "But now they're making personal appearances in the dreams of Samantha O'Malley. There's a title for a TV show. 'The Dreams of Samantha O'Malley.'"

She grabbed his wrist. "That's right. I just remembered. That was the one consistent thing in all these dreams—it was the magpie! I was a jaguar, a polar bear, a wolf, a giraffe—I was any number of animals, but every time a yellow-billed magpie would come swooping down, and I'd drop everything to follow it."

"Well, Samantha O'Malley—that yellow-billed magpie was leading you home. That ought to tell you something."

She stared at him in amazement. "Yeah, maybe. Maybe that's what the dreams are about. Except—I don't know."

"What?"

"I've been having these dreams for a while, certainly while I was living in the foothills. But I did come home, I'm here now. So why am I still having them? They've actually increased. I'm having them more than ever now."

He chuckled and shrugged. "That's a mystery even for Mister E," he intoned in mock solemnity. He glanced at the clock on the nightstand. "Look, babe, I've got to get going soon. I've got a date to go hiking with Dale." He kissed her again, more slowly. "Hey, you want to come with us?"

"No, of course not. That's your time with your son; I don't want to interfere with that."

"Sam, you know Dale would love to see you."

"Gee, Charlie, I'd like to see him too, but I'm not going to spring myself on him—and you shouldn't spring me on him either." She turned away and reached for her robe. "We don't even know what we're doing here, Mystery."

He rubbed her back. "We're two old friends getting reacquainted, Sam. Nothing wrong with that."

She gave him a doleful look. "I know, baby. But at some point, we're two old friends who need to talk, you know? I mean, are we just delaying a repeat of that inevitable conversation we already had? When was it?--about five, six years ago?"

"Maybe it'll be different this time, Sam."

"Yeah, I know, we're both different people, right?" She couldn't hide a hint of sarcasm in her voice. She got up, and seeing herself in her dresser mirror, she ran her fingers through her hair and licked her lips, as if she were getting ready to audition for a part in a play.

"I know," Charlie said, taking her hand and twirling her round like a jitterbug dancer. "The Sam doesn't like things to happen too fast for her. She likes to sit in a cool and quiet shady spot, doing a little contemplation before she decides to take action. But every now and then, Mystery shows up and she doesn't think, she just starts kissing him."

She laughed and pulled away from him. "How do you fit that head of yours through the doorway, Mister E!"

"Go take a shower," he told her. "I'll make breakfast."

He made her a hearty breakfast of scrambled eggs with spinach, tomatoes and coriander seeds. "Talk to you soon," he said in his noncommittal way as he dashed out the door. He gave her a long lingering kiss, but left her kitchen in a mess. Same old Mister E, she thought, as she washed the dishes and mopped the kitchen floor. Yep, that was the man she had fallen in love with. He was the guy.

He had fallen into her life as her teaching career hit its stride. She'd been teaching six years, and she felt established and confident in her abilities. She had moved to a different school with a more supportive principal in a better neighborhood. She had a nice classroom, not a portable trailer on stilts. Her aides were friendly and supportive, fun to work with. The other teachers were happy to include her special education students. She was content in life. She had let go of her desire to have a special spiritual mission. She was just a woman doing her work. Nothing special, and she was satisfied with that.

Then her principal called her to the office one day and told her a man had called wanting to volunteer his time to put in a school garden. He seemed nice enough, just a man from the neighborhood, who'd passed by the school and wanted to do something nice for the kids and the community. "He said he liked the energy here," the principal said to Samantha, and Samantha's ears had pricked up. This was Craig-speak. She hadn't heard from Craig in three years, but she was always looking for some manifestation of Craig, someone who spoke his language, someone who might recognize her too as a kindred spirit, someone she might feel a connection to.

"I thought of your students right away," the principal told Samantha. "I thought this would be a good project for them." He extended his hand, gave her a slip of paper with a name and number on it. "Why don't you give him a call, see if you can work something out with this guy."

So Samantha had called the number left by Charlie Easter, but it turned out to be a message phone, the number of a coffee house in a neighboring community. Samantha didn't care: she'd dealt with volunteers before; they weren't always the most reliable people.

But it got her thinking about it all. A school garden over in that space between the portables and the levee that supported the railroad tracks. It was just around the corner from her classroom. It would be a good spot, and the kids would have so much fun. Samantha realized she'd never even been over there. It looked like it was covered with waist high weeds; that might be more than she could deal with. But she should check it out. See if it could be salvaged.

She made a point of getting up early one Friday morning, of driving over to the school early to check the place out. It was early October, a touch of crispness in the early fall air. She brought an extra pair of shoes because certainly it would be damp in the weeds.

She strode over behind the buildings in her full denim skirt and her hiking boots. She felt as if she were on an adventure, sneaking out past the other early bird teachers who were occupied in their quiet classrooms. She pushed the unlatched gate back and stepped carefully amid Bermuda runners and nut grass. It was a big area; she wondered where the best spot would be to start. She allowed herself a fantasy of a full-blown garden with fruit trees and fountains, an oasis within this concrete urban landscape. She was pacing slowly, gazing into space, not really paying such close attention to where her feet might fall, when suddenly her toe tapped against something solid, though too soft to be a rock. She glanced down casually and her heart leapt into her throat: her toe was brushing against a man's denim calf. She leapt back in startled distress, audibly gasping in fright. The man's eyes flew open, and he sat up.

"Good morning," he announced, as if he were a mechanical doll that spoke when prodded. He pulled back his blanket and leapt to his feet. "I'm sorry; I didn't mean to scare you." Back then his brown hair was thick and wavy. He was thin with high cheekbones.

She stepped back further. "What are you doing here?" she asked, shielding her eyes from the rising sun. "Have you been sleeping here?"

"No, of course not, I mean not always, not every night." He looked a little frantic, though certainly clean and recently shaved.

She stepped back again, unsure, but no longer nervous. "You know," she said, trying to be friendly, "this is not a good place to sleep. If you're caught here—I mean, well, there's no telling what people might think. You know what I'm saying, don't you? This is school property, and you shouldn't be sleeping on school property."

"But I wasn't here all night," he said defensively.

"Look, I won't say anything, but you see what I'm saying, don't you? This is a school—you wouldn't want people to think—look, you wouldn't want people to think you're a pedophile. Okay? I said it, all right? I think you better leave, before too many people show up. Okay?" She continued to back away, not turning her back on him, stepping cautiously away.

But then he grinned at her and she got her first look at his magical crinkly-eyed smile. She didn't know it then but for years she would carry this mental snapshot of him, that first impression: he seemed a creature of the morning light, rose-gold skin and amber eyes. In that moment she had to smile back, despite her better judgment. She couldn't stop herself.

"I didn't scare you, did I?" he asked.

"Wow," she said, "don't you get it? You are asking the wrong questions! It doesn't matter if you scared me or not. Just leave, okay?"

"Okay, I will," he said as if making a solemn promise. "So do you teach here?"

"Yes, and if you don't leave now, I'm going to go get the principal and the custodian, and maybe the police."

"No, you're not," he said, still smiling. "You can tell I'm not causing any trouble. You can tell. You know people and you can tell."

She stared at him. "Why do you say that?"

"I don't know. It just feels right. You're probably the art teacher or the music teacher or—hey, maybe you're the special ed teacher. You just have this aura around you, you're a little more sensitive than other people. It just feels that way to me."

She was at the gate, thinking she should walk through, back to her regular ordinary world, where things were more predictable maybe, where men weren't sleeping in the weeds. But she lingered there on this side of the gate, not sure what to say, not sure she should say anything. "You're very intuitive," she told him. "But for your sake—I still think you should leave." She glanced at her watch. "I need to get going. My students will be here soon."

"You're right, I'll leave. But hey--" He extended his hand. "I'm Charlie Easter."

"Oh, you're the man who wants to put in the garden."

"That's right." He stepped toward her, still holding out his hand. She finally accepted it, shook it politely. "Samantha O'Malley," she said.

"Ms O'Malley," he said formally, "it's good to meet you." She nodded but he did not let go of her hand. "This would make a fine garden," he said, launching into what appeared to be a sales pitch. "It gets a lot of sun, and the soil is good. This used to be flood plain before they put in the levee. It's a good spot."

She pulled away from him. "So you were just here checking out the soil, huh?"

He nodded. "I was. That's what I've been doing. I woke up early and I came over here around four, just to see the sun rise over these slick green weeds here. But I lay down and fell asleep. Really."

His lips were curling and she couldn't help it, she hated herself for it, but she couldn't stop smiling. "Look," she said. "This will be our secret. And you better not come back until you're looking a little more respectable, or my principal will have a cow and a half."

"Whoa!" he exclaimed. "Not just a full cow, but the full cow and an extra half cow! Well, I do not want to mess with that!" She rolled her eyes; he continued. "What are you twelve?—imitating Bart Simpson?"

"Oh, Mr. Easter, you're quite the comedian."

He laughed. "You don't have to call me Mr. Easter; call me Charlie. Even the kids call me Mr. E."

"Mr. E," she said thoughtfully, "because you're quite the

mystery."

"Exactly," he agreed. "And Ms O'Malley, I suspect I will be calling you Ms Omm." He posed his hands into a contemplative yogic mudra.

"What?"

"Ms Omm!" he exclaimed. "O-m for O'Malley—or ommmm—you know, because speaking with you has put me in a bliss state."

She laughed, despite feeling embarrassed. "I'm leaving now."

He lingered at the gate. "I'll be back this afternoon to help you with the garden!" he called after her.

***

A pyramid had somehow sprouted in Samantha's atrium. Cross-legged in a perfect lotus position, her eyes half closed and her hands held gently on her knees, palms up, thumbs upon her middle fingers, she breathed deeply into her belly.

I celebrate myself, and sing myself,

And what I assume you shall assume,

For every atom belonging to me as good belongs to you.

The Whitman lines drifted through her mind as if the poem were a breeze, gentle and unbidden. She was content.

A flurry of wings brushed against her cheek and ear. She opened her eyes, unsurprised to find a yellow-billed magpie hovering at her side. "Welcome," she said aloud. The bird lit on her shoulder, and she felt herself ease deeper into a blissful trance state. Do you have a message for me? *she asked the bird without words.*

Yes, came the throbbing response, yes. Nom meoho renge keo. The words pulsed at the base of her spine, and then drifted through her womb, her solar plexus, her heart, her throat, her third eye and up to the crown of her head. Nom meoho renge keo. It didn't seem to come from the bird but through it. The energy was irresistible, and she felt herself vibrating faster to match it, so fast, so fast, it was almost scary, because her body was becoming thinner and thinner, like hot soup as it approaches a boil, and she feared she would turn into steam and disappear into the air, so fast was she vibrating, faster and faster, until she felt her heart tearing open, tearing open to burst. An orgasmic wave flowed out through her heart through her throat and belly. She called out Charlie's name, or maybe she only thought she did, but then she awoke, and she was lying in bed staring at the play of moonlight on the ceiling.

CHAPTER ELEVEN

On Tuesday Samantha held Lulu in from recess to try facilitated communication with her. She hadn't tried the technique with anyone for nearly 12 years; she had no idea what would happen. Would it be a waste of time? She had prepared a few worksheets on her lap top computer over the weekend; now she seated Lulu beside her as she brought up the document on the screen.

What was she getting herself into here? Lulu's mother had been willing to bring in some professor from Syracuse; why hadn't she let her do that? You lose all reason around this subject, she scolded herself.

She took Lulu's hand, but the girl resisted. She held her firmly, despite her struggle, and she folded back the girl's middle, ring and pinkie fingers as she used to do. This left the index finger free to act as pointer. Wasn't there some little nursery rhyme about that? Where is pointer? Here I am. Here I am. She blinked and swallowed to get herself back on track.

"Calm yourself, Lulu," Samantha said soothingly. "Trust me; this is going to be fun." The girl continued to rock in her chair, but she stopped trying to pull her hand away.

"Okay, kiddo," she began, "I'm going to ask you some questions." She paused for a moment, then turned in her seat. Lulu seldom made eye contact with her or with anyone else. Samantha gently but deliberately held Lulu's face so she could look into her eyes. "Lulu, I know you're in there," she said in a firm but quiet voice. "I want you to focus: I want to teach you a new way to communicate. But it will take hard work. I need you to know that you already know how to do this. I'm going to guide you at first, but you will remember what to do. You already know, okay?"

She was glad the room was empty because she knew there were those among her colleagues who would scoff at her efforts to talk to Lulu as if she were an intelligent and alert child. What if she were wrong? Well, no harm done, right? But what if she were right? Well, that could change everything, couldn't it? She took a deep breath.

"Here's the first question, sweetie," she pointed to the computer screen. "Can you see that? What do you think?"

The question read, "Do you like ice cream?" but Samantha didn't want to read it aloud. She wanted to know if Lulu could read it and give a reasonable answer. She pointed Lulu's hand toward the keyboard. "So read the question, and type an answer, Lulu." She sat as Lulu rocked, but the girl didn't move her hand. Samantha moved Lulu's hand closer for her, but still Lulu rocked her body, staring hypnotically at the computer screen. Time to take the assistance up a notch.

"See Luisa," Samantha started again. "See—it says 'do you like ice cream?' Do you? Do you like ice cream?" Lulu squawked loudly. "Well, sweetie, I know you like ice cream because I've seen you eat ice cream!" Samantha said insistently. "I think we can safely say you like ice cream." She paused. "So you can type your response to that." Again she waited, holding Lulu's hand as she rocked. "Any time, Lulu, any time," she said in a barely audible voice. She looked away up at the ceiling, wondering how she had done this years ago. Why had it worked back then?

Years ago, it had seemed like magic. At first she hadn't been able to convince the children that this was a viable option. But once she'd had the break-through with Jim, everything had fallen into place. It was easy!

She recalled the day that Lam showed up in her classroom. His family had arrived from Vietnam only months earlier, and Lam had been bounced from general education to the resource program to a special day class for students with mild learning handicaps, and finally the powers-that-be had sent him to Samantha. He was like a small feral animal, arriving midmorning to stare at the other children in fright. He screamed in distress, a loud, guttural yap, wordless, but not without meaning. Samantha sent the other kids out early for recess. Lam hid under a table.

She took a portable keyboard, a small electronic dictionary that was generally used to correct spelling errors. She crawled under the table after him and extended her hand. He moved away from her, but she was persistent. She had him trapped by the wall, and he surrendered to her touch. "Can you tell me your name?" she asked him, and he started to type. There was no hesitation, no reluctance. He typed quickly and confidently.

"I am Lam after my uncle Lam killed in war. I not remember him, but father remembers. They in prison together. When my father out we come here. Come on boat, dark dark at night, but I not scared, not scared. I happy father mother say we come safe place. But I not feel safe here. Not all time."

He stopped and stared at her, pulling his hand away. Just as suddenly he reached forward and grabbed her hand to resume typing. "Strange." Again he dropped her hand, jumped up from the floor and ran across the room. He stood near the door and looked back at her.

"You may not leave this room," she told him firmly. Then she realized that she had sounded harsh, and she amended her tone. "You don't know your way around the school yet. When you learn your way around, you may leave with permission. This rule is for safety. You understand that."

He took a step toward her and she approached him slowly. He met her halfway in the middle of the room. At that moment he had taken her hand willingly and begun to type again. "Scary. Never before. You know me. Strange scary strange."

Now Samantha stared at Lulu, and thought of Lam. How could I have done that back then? How could I have helped him do that so easily? Or was it all me? Was I creating this story that he told me? Was it really my story?

No, she told herself. She knew he had approached her, even that first time. He had reached for her hand, he had been eager to communicate, to be known for the first time. She couldn't have been guiding his hand. It had to have been genuine.

She tightened her grip on Lulu's hand. "Let me show you, Lulu. This is how you type the word yes." She guided her finger to the Y key, to the E, to the S. "That's how it's done. Now you know, so you can do it yourself." Lulu squealed and pulled away. The bell rang.

Samantha sent a note to Anna. "I tried facilitating with Luisa today without success. Let's try it for a week, and then regroup. You can call in your professors then if you want."

An hour after the kids had left, there was a sharp rap at the classroom door. Adam Yang was delivering another pie. "Pecan!" he said. "That's all, just pecan."

"I love pecan," Samantha said cheerfully.

"Ms Villaseñor says she's very pleased that you're making an effort with Luisa. She says to keep her posted."

"Will do,'" Samantha promised. "Tell her I'll send daily reports, but she can't send pies every day. I don't want to appear ungrateful—they've been great--but I'll be bigger than a house by Halloween at this rate."

***

Samantha took few breaks this week, spending every free minute with Lulu, attempting to teach her to type. Was that what she was doing? She didn't really know. She didn't tell anyone what she was doing, afraid of backlash and ridicule, being accused of misleading a parent. Didn't matter, there was nothing anyone could suspect her of. After all, she was getting nowhere. She spent her recess watching Lulu rock and rock, but nothing else happened. Nothing.

She went home every evening alone, wondering each night if she'd hear from Charlie. The days slipped by without a word from him. This was typical, she reminded herself. He seemed to live in a different dimension where time passed at a different rate of speed than everywhere else on the planet. Or perhaps it was just here in California that he had created this little pocket of an alternative universe. A different time and space that she could not enter unless he gave her the key, and he seldom remembered that no one else had that key.

***

On Thursday, a chatty substitute teacher showed up in the staff room. Chubby and flamboyant in a gauzy floral print dress she cornered Samantha by the microwave oven. "I love your earrings," she gushed as Samantha waited for her leftover meat loaf to heat up.

"Thank you," Samantha said curtly, unhappy to be drawn away from her private ruminations about Lulu and Charlie.

"Are they turquoise?" she persisted.

"No, they're jade."

"Oh, my goodness, did you get them in Asia?"

"No, from a shop in midtown. On sale."

"So beautiful."

Hannah Bank, the brand new second grade teacher, walked in wearing green and white checked canvas loafers, and the chatty sub lost interest in Samantha's earrings. "Wow, look at those! Those really take me back!" She waylaid Hannah by the door, speaking in a voice loud enough to draw every eye in the room. "I remember seeing those back in the 80s. They're so retro and yet so classic! Of course you were probably barely out of diapers when I was wearing those across campus at UC Berkeley. God, those were the days."

Hannah seemed a bit embarrassed by the sub's attention. But Samantha felt mesmerized by the busy pattern on the shoes too. The sub was on to some story about her college days while Hannah stood staring at her, an awkward smile frozen on her young face.

Samantha took the opportunity to sneak out. She ate quickly in her classroom, then retrieved Lulu from the playground.

"Lulu," she asked, "did you see Ms Bank's shoes today? Let's go take a peek." She led Lulu down the hall to the second grade room, where Hannah sat at her desk eating a sandwich and perusing a math textbook. "Hey Hannah, this is Luisa," Samantha told the young teacher. "I think Luisa would like your shoes."

"Really?" Hannah asked in a serious tone.

"I know it's weird," Samantha conceded in a soft tone, "but could you just stretch your feet out from behind your desk and let Lulu get a look at them?"

Hannah laughed. "Okay." She obliged the odd request, as Samantha led Lulu closer to her feet.

"Check out the shoes, Lulu. Aren't they a kick?"

Lulu stared at the geometric pattern and squealed. She pulled away from Samantha to push her face closer and closer down to the green and white checks. "What is she doing?" Hannah asked, surprised.

Samantha shrugged. "She's 'stimming'—or stimulating herself—on the geometric pattern on your shoes. All people with autism do it to an extent. They stare at lights or moving fan blades or their own hands." She waved her spread fingers a few inches in front of her own eyes to demonstrate. "It relaxes them or excites them— but always it distracts them."

"Like a trance state, maybe?" Hannah asked.

"Yes, exactly!" Samantha affirmed and it struck her how much she enjoyed meditating. In some ways maybe 'stimming' wasn't much different. "The difference I guess," she mused, "is that Lulu gets stuck when she's stimming. She doesn't seem to have control. It's hard to get her out of it, and back to the real world."

Hannah looked quizzical. "So you wanted to see if my shoes would send Lulu into a trance?"

Samantha laughed. "Let's just say I'd forgotten something and your shoes reminded me, that's all."

"Okay—uh—can I help you with anything else?"

"No, I'm sorry to disturb you, but this was helpful to me."

Hannah laughed. "Anytime, Sam. Bring your kids by anytime! It's always interesting!"

Samantha led Lulu back to the classroom. "You've been stimming on the light of the computer screen, haven't you, Lulu?" The girl squealed. Samantha looked at her, wishing she could trust this vocalization to be confirmation of her suspicion, but there was no way of knowing. "We need an old style typewriter," she announced as they entered the classroom. She sunk down into a chair at the table and Lulu readily sat beside her. "There are just too many sensory distractions with a computer." She rested her chin in her hand. "I got rid of my old typewriters a couple of moves ago!"

She paused to stare at the girl, rocking again, still rocking. "Wait a minute." She jumped up and rushed across the room. She grabbed a piece of graph paper and brought it over to the table. With a black felt pen and a ruler, she drew a keyboard on it. She had all the letters, but not all the numbers. She glanced at the clock. Five minutes till the bell. This would have to do for now. She picked up Lulu's hand. "This is a little more primitive than a computer but it works just the same. See--" she pointed with her own fingers— "here's the Y, the E, the S. And you could spell 'NO' here too. It's easy." She paused to stare at the girl, but Lulu would not make eye contact. "Okay, Luisa, my dear: new question—what did you think of Ms Bank's shoes? Did you like them?"

Samantha tightened her grip on Lulu's hand. Lulu looked at the paper keyboard and reached forward, her index finger like a knife, jabbing into space. She hit the Y, she hit the E she hit the S. YES, she signaled. YES, VERY COOL.

***

At the end of September, the staff hosted a farewell party for principal Jon Convivio, who was retiring on his 65th birthday. In a week he would be heading off to Washington state to live on an island on Puget Sound with his daughter and her family. There were lots of fishing jokes and gifts of warm clothes and gloves. The veteran teachers who had been at the school the longest got up and told exaggerated tales of students that Jon had saved from the twin evils of laziness and piss poor attitude. There were gentle insults, and sweet memories of Jon's wife Sylvia who had died of breast cancer three years earlier.

As a relative newcomer to the staff, Samantha sat at the back of the rented room at the Firehouse in Old Sacramento with the secretary, the health aide and a few of the intermediate teachers and their spouses. She watched the other teachers with their partners and felt lonely, thinking of Tom, thinking of Charlie. "Rebecca," she said, leaning toward the school secretary during a lull in conversation. "I'm thinking I may have to take a day off next week for a dental appointment. Do you think we could get Mr. Easter to sub in my room? He comes and helps them out at recess sometimes and he's really good with them. Do you think that might work out?"

"Oh, he's gone, Samantha. He's not subbing anymore."

"What?"

"Yeah, he called the district office last week and said he had to leave town, and he won't be back for a while. I don't know when he'll be available again."

She leaned forward, hoping no one would hear about this inordinate interest she had in Charlie Easter. "Why did he leave town? I mean—he, uh--" she stopped herself, not willing to admit a knowledge of Charlie's son and Charlie's plot at the community garden and Charlie's job at the Co-op grocery store where he guided members and other customers through the soup and salad bar one evening a week and one Saturday a month.

"I don't know, Samantha. But we could get Bev Ann Knox; she used to teach resource at Earl Warren Middle School. She's retired now, but she likes to pick up a few jobs a month and she likes the special ed classes."

"Yeah," Samantha said, feigning interest in this prospective sub. "I'll check in with you on Monday about this. You know, if I do decide to take a day off. Maybe I'll be able to get an appointment after three. I'll let you know."

"Whatever you need, Samantha," Rebecca nodded.

As the evening ended, Samantha approached the retiring

principal and shook his hand. "I know we haven't known each other long, but I've really enjoyed working with you," she said sincerely.

"Hey, you got me at a good time. It's so great to stop caring!" He gave a hearty laugh, and she laughed a bit too.

"Oh, I don't believe that, Mr. C!"

"No, I'm joking; it's not that I don't care about the kids—not that at all. In fact, this year, I've been so close to the end that I just blew off all those dumb ass administrative hot shots at the district office that I've had to kow tow to for years. Finally I just focused on the children. I promised myself I would do that. That was my present to myself. I haven't been able to do that to this extent, not since the new guard came in ten or twelve years ago—but I did it this semester. Don't look for it again, my dear. You shall not see my like again."

"Look for this chivalry only in books, for tis gone with the wind!" she said with a dramatic flourish.

He clicked his heels together and gave a short bow to her. "Ah, Scarlet, tis true—and frankly my dear--"

"Oh please don't say it," she said with mock pique, "I couldn't bear it."

He laughed. "Come have a drink with us. Some of us are going to have one more drink in the bar, Samantha."

"Thank you, but I should be going."

"One drink, Ms O'Malley....."

"And I'll be asleep at the wheel, Mr. Convivio."

"Hey, I'll drive you home. You live near the school, right?"

"And then I'll have to take a cab to get my car in the morning..."

"Or," he said, bending close to her ear, "I could drive you to my home, and then I'll drive you back here in the morning!"

She stepped back a bit shocked, and yet flattered. "You are quite the rogue, Mr. C!" she scolded.

"Forgive me, Samantha, but I've been a widower for too long. Sylvia made it very clear before she died that she did not want me to be lonely. And on occasion, I haven't been." He paused to gauge her reaction, but she merely nodded. "I like you, Samantha; you're a beautiful young woman."

"I ain't so young," she protested.

He shook his head, dismissing her self-deprecating remark. "All I'm saying is that next week I'll be on my way to Washington state, and if you'd like to join me in a fond farewell, you are welcome. If not, I hope I have flattered, rather than insulted you, with my invitation. I meant no harm."

"I am flattered," she assured him. "In fact I'm touched. Thank you."

"You're welcome," he lifted her hand and kissed it gently. "Well, there are others waiting in the bar."

"Well, we better not keep them waiting, Jon," she said taking his arm. "But I'm switching to Sprite."

He grinned. "A wise move. Perhaps I should do the same."

CHAPTER TWELVE

"So what do we do now?" Anna asked Samantha.

"Um, well--" Samantha tapped her pen on an open notebook page, trying to think what to say. I DON'T KNOW!!! That's what she wanted to blurt out, but stammering seemed a better alternative to an admission of ignorance. "I think we definitely need an old fashioned typewriter," she said slowly. "Lulu spent too much time stimming on the light of the computer screen. It distracted her from typing."

"Lulu?" Anna repeated with a cocked eyebrow.

Samantha felt herself blush. "We call her Lulu. I don't know how that got started, but it stuck. We can go back to Luisa if you'd prefer."

"Well, of course I prefer Luisa," Anna said slowly. "But perhaps you should ask Luisa what she prefers!"

Samantha smiled. "I like your attitude," she said. "It is time for us to realize that Luisa will now have some opinions of her own. But don't lose sight of the fact that Luisa is a child, and we are the grown-ups, and we still have to make decisions for her."

"Well, of course," Anna said, seemingly a little annoyed at such a simplistic suggestion.

"No, I'm sorry," Samantha said quickly. "I've just seen this happen before—parents who are so excited to know what their formerly silent kids are thinking, and before you know it, the kids are ruling the roost."

"So you have done this before?" Anna said, with a coy smile, seeming a little smug that Samantha had tipped her hand.

Samantha felt almost sick that she had revealed something. "It was a long time ago."

"And the media did not treat you kindly; I know." Anna opened her own notebook. "You don't have to apologize to me or tell me sad tales. I've always sensed that Luisa was in there." She quickly jotted "typewriter" on her pad. "I don't know where one goes to get a typewriter these days, but my people will track one down for you."

"And one for you, Anna," Samantha interjected. "You should be facilitating with Luisa at home."

"I want to! You'll show me how."

"Of course. It's not hard. I can show you right now if you want."

"In a minute. Samantha, I want to know—should Luisa be placed in a different classroom now? A room where they're focusing on a more academic agenda? Perhaps even fully included in an age appropriate general education classroom?"

Samantha took a deep breath. She did not relish the thought of discussing this with her program specialist or new principal. "I don't know, Anna. Facilitated communication was discredited years ago; if I call my administrators and say I'm doing this with your daughter—even at your request—there's no telling what they might say. Maybe they'll tell me to stop; I don't know. I'm willing to keep going at this point, but we need verification that what I've experienced with Luisa is legitimate. If you start typing with her and we're able to establish some reliability—some consistency between the girl you communicate with and the one I communicate with—then we can make an argument to place her in any program you want."

"But you aren't guiding her hand, are you? You're sure of that, aren't you?" Anna's tone was rather sharp as if she were asking a subordinate about why they had bought flour at such a high price—hadn't they checked all the markets? Samantha took a deep breath.

"Anna—I'm not going to sugar coat this—I don't know! We had a small success last Friday. Do I think it was genuine? Yes! But it's new for both Luisa and me. This will take some time." She paused, and Anna nodded.

"I see what you're saying; we need to be cautious."

"Exactly," Samantha agreed. "We need to show validity and reliability. We need proof. And we need time for both Luisa and us to become comfortable with this process. After that, well, then I guess it would be time for me to give Luisa some rigorous academic testing to see where she comes out. But of course, results of any testing may be suspect. People will wonder who's really taking the test—Luisa or Samantha! And to be honest—I wouldn't even be sure."

"Samantha, I don't know what happened in the past to spook you and make you overly cautious, but once we establish reliability, then any results of testing will be viewed as valid, won't they? I don't see why we should worry about that."

"Anna, I--" She paused, wondering how to explain. "Well, for example, if you and Lulu go to San Francisco over the weekend, and then she comes to school and types to me that the two of you had lunch at Fisherman's Wharf, and then you saw the Lion King in a theater and spent the night at the Hyatt Hotel!" She exhaled a deep breath after making this big list. "And then I call you up, and you confirm it all: yes, everything Lulu told you happened, we did all that—well of course we know that Lulu is actually communicating through the facilitation, and we can feel good about that! Lulu will have shown us that she is able to talk to us both, and won't that be amazing! But!" She paused for emphasis. "When it comes time for testing, can I be sure of the same validity? I know the answers on the test. Can I be sure I'm not guiding her hand? I mean, in the same way—if I knew you two went to San Francisco, could I be sure that I didn't guide her hand when I asked her to tell me about it? Do you see what I mean?"

"Yes, I see exactly what you mean. This isn't easy, is it?"

Samantha felt a deep heaviness in her chest, and for a quick moment she thought she might burst into tears.

"Samantha," Anna said slowly. "Maybe you'll think I'm crazy. But I just have this feeling that Luisa is trapped in a body that won't function the way she wants it to. It's so painful sometimes to see the look on her face. I'm sure she wants to tell me something, but neither one of us can break through this terrible barrier." She stopped speaking abruptly folding her hands in front of herself, staring at her fingernails. "I wonder if autism is akin to something like Parkinson's disease. Obviously this isn't my area of expertise, but, well--"

Samantha quickly put her hand on top of the other woman's. "Neurology is certainly not my area of expertise either, but I'm with you! There is more going on with these kids than we can possibly know--"

The classroom door swung open suddenly and the custodian's bulky cart noisily preceded its owner into the room. It was not the usual custodian who stuck his head in after it. On seeing the two women at the front table, the man backed out quickly. "Sorry," he said abruptly. He left the cart, but closed the door behind himself.

Samantha half stood; the man had looked so familiar. But he was gone, and she had a visitor. "Um, I'm sorry; I forgot what we were saying—umm--"

"That's okay; I need to get going anyway," Anna said quickly, seemingly a bit embarrassed that she had dropped her professional demeanor for a moment or two. "So let's recap: I will get two typewriters so we can both begin facilitation with Luisa. The main goal at this time will be to establish comfort and rapport for Luisa, as well as reliability, particularly by eliciting information from her that one of us could not know, but that the other could verify as accurate."

"Exactly," Samantha nodded.

"After that, there is the question of how to establish validity in academic testing," Anna continued, jotting quick notes.

"Well, that's when we'll have to work on fading out the support,"

Samantha said. "It's the only way we can be completely sure."

"You're right of course," Anna acknowledged. "I do realize that." She closed her notebook. Doodles of pyramids graced the cover. Samantha couldn't help but stare at them.

Anna pulled up her massive leather purse, and proceeded to close up shop. Meeting adjourned. She stood quickly and extended her hand to Samantha. "This is going to be a very fruitful partnership," Anna declared with a smile. "I knew it from the first time we met. You don't waste time, Samantha. I like that."

Samantha smiled wanly, thinking Anna could fill one of those pyramid-covered notebooks with all the things she "liked." These compliments always seemed laden with expectations. They didn't leave Samantha with a feeling of warmth or reassurance.

"So," Anna grinned in conclusion, "are you sure I can't convince you to accept another pie?" She laughed. "I know I can be a bit overwhelming in my generosity at times."

"Oh, I don't mean that you should never give me another pie!" Samantha exclaimed. "A life without Anna Victoria's pies would be too sad to contemplate. But please—none today. I had a very calorie-laden weekend."

Anna shrugged. "As you wish. But watch your calories next weekend, because the new harvest pies will debut a week from today. You won't want to miss them."

Samantha slouched in her chair after Anna left. She felt anxious, and was actually disappointed that a pie wasn't on the way. She sat up, grabbing her lesson plan book to see when she could plan times to facilitate with Lulu. She couldn't keep giving up breaks. "I'm going to have to tell my aides what I'm doing with her," she said aloud. The two women probably had never even heard of FC, Samantha realized. They probably wouldn't even care. She stood up. "You worry too much," she told a smiling scarecrow that graced the center of the front board. "About way too many things."

She had had a lovely time Saturday night/Sunday morning with Jon Convivio, and then they had said good-bye. Essentially a one night stand. No, she heard her internal critic scold, stop being so hard on yourself, it wasn't a one night stand. It was two consenting adults who knew each other well enough to enjoy an evening together. And there were no expectations. The invitation had been issued and accepted in that spirit. No expectations, no surprises. And so what if Charlie Easter had left town. Typical Charlie Easter behavior. Maybe she'd hear from him again, maybe she wouldn't.

"Stop holding me to such impossibly high standards!" she told the scarecrow, since there was no one else in the room to berate. "I am simply telling the universe that I am ready to welcome new experiences into my life. I am moving on from Tom to the next thing—whatever that may be." And yet, a nagging worry played at her. Was she taking a step forward or back? Here she was again, facilitating with a student, against her better judgment, and worse yet, sleeping with Charlie Easter! This was not the way she had expected her new life back in the valley to go. But even the valley wasn't new. Maybe she had made a mistake coming back here. She sank back down into a chair.

The door swung open and the guest custodian stuck his head inside. "Is the coast clear?" she heard him call.

She stood up. "Sure, c'mon in."

A wave of warm air rushed up her torso and face as she watched the newcomer drag a vacuum cleaner to the far side of the room. He was balding and he'd put on more than a few pounds, but there was no mistaking her old friend. His face was unlined serenity, even as he reached for a mop, but Samantha had to grip the edge of the table to steady herself. *Was it really him?* "Craig?" she asked, saying his name softly.

The tall man turned, his eyes narrowed in curiosity, the corners of his lips lifted optimistically. Samantha held her breath. *Didn't he remember her?* But then he snorted with a quick chuckle of surprise. His face spread into a wide grin, laugh lines fanning across his jaw and temples. "Samantha!" he exclaimed. "How good to see you!"

Still she stood, too awed to move. She cleared her throat. "What are you doing here?"

He laughed, tipping his head back as if she'd just said the funniest thing in the world. "I was wondering that too!" he declared.

"What am I doing at this school? But it's obvious now, Samantha: I'm here to see you!"

CHAPTER THIRTEEN

She started toward him and they met in the center of the room. She reached up to embrace him and he pulled her into his sheltering chest. She felt him bending as his lips brushed the top of her head, then he stepped away quickly. Samantha knew there was no romance in his gesture. No, his kiss was a blessing, a deliberate transfer of grace. She glanced downward, suddenly feeling shy, but he craned his neck to meet her gaze. "I have a message for you," he said.

She nearly gasped. "A message? For me?"

He spread his arms. "It must be for you. You're the only one here!"

She laughed at his sassy retort, reminded of the way he used to read her mind and her mood, dealing out the perfect joke or aphorism at the proper time like a winning card in Black Jack. And what Puckish delight he used to take in her unabashed surprise. She'd been like a kid, eager to hear the next punch line—and that hadn't changed. "So tell me," she said.

"It has to do with progress," he told her. "It's like a slingshot." She narrowed her eyes and stared in confusion at him. He continued. "A slingshot," he repeated. "You have to pull it back before it can propel you forward."

"Okay," she said slowly. "But what does that mean?"

"I don't know," he admitted. "I'm just the messenger. I assumed it would have some meaning for you."

She shrugged.

He set his mouth into a serious thin line. "Well, Samantha," he said, "sometimes it seems we're going backwards when we really want to move forward. But if we back up a little, pull the slingshot back, it gives us the momentum to propel ourselves forward at a much greater speed." He paused. "Does that make more sense now?"

"Oh," she said softly as she lowered herself into the nearest chair, which happened to be at Echo's desk. Her eyes welled up. "How do you do that?" she squeaked. "It's exactly what I wanted to hear."

She pressed her hands over her eyes as tears began to slide down her cheeks, but she could feel him moving away. He returned a moment later with a box of Kleenex that he plopped on her lap. "I hate it when I have this kind of effect on women," he said. "They all seem to start crying when they see me coming. How do you think this makes poor Craig feel? Not great for his ego, let me tell you."

A sharp rap on the front door made Samantha dry her tears quickly. Adam Yang looked almost apologetic. "Ms Villaseñor wanted you to have this because it's a seasonal pie that will be discontinued for the winter next week. She says it freezes well if you prefer."

"What is it?"

"Triple berry; great a la mode."

***

"Sorry we don't have any ice cream," Samantha told Craig as she passed him a slice of the pie.

"Hey, no complaints here. Though I would like a fork."

"Hold your horses." She hurried to the back of the room to pull two forks out of a drawer by the sink. She returned with forks, napkins and her own piece of pie plated. "To old friends," she said lifting her fork to him in a toast.

"To the energy which brings us back together," he said with a nod.

"Oh, my God!" she exclaimed as she took a bite. "This is the best one yet!" She dabbed at her mouth with a Halloween napkin. "This woman is going to drive me crazy."

"Who? The woman who keeps sending you pies? Sounds like a good deal to me. I hope I can keep this job long term, now that I see there are fringe benefits."

"Gee, it's not enough to see me again?" she countered, then she began to tear up again. "You disappeared on me. Why do men always disappear on me?"

He stared at her as he chewed a large mouthful of pastry and fruit, again passing her the Kleenex. He swallowed. "I don't know, Samantha. Why do *you* think men disappear on you?"

"I don't know!"

"It's not that you aren't lovable, because you are," he said taking another bite, seemingly unconcerned with her sniffling beside him. "But when you can't find what you want externally—well, what do you think the universe is trying to tell you?"

She blew her nose. "I don't know."

"C'mon, Samantha; this is supposed to be a dialogue here, a little Socratic interplay—I mean, the answer was practically contained in the question. It's a no-brainer."

"What was the question?"

He laughed heartily, though this did not distract him from the pie. "Eat your pie, Samantha. Everything in the universe comes into clearer focus when you're eating pie. Your priorities become clear and the path to bliss opens before you."

She dutifully took a bite. "This is so good," she whimpered, then she leaned back in her chair and cleared her throat. "I don't know what is the matter with me today. I am so weepy." She shuddered as if shaking dust from her shoulders, elbows, and lap, then took a deep breath. "I'm okay," she said unconvincingly. "I've just felt a little shaky today. Was kind of nauseated this morning, and now I feel sore all over."

"Do you have a fever?"

"No, no it's nothing like that. I'm just a little stressed."

He took his last bite of the pie. "Maybe you're pregnant." He licked his fork. "Do you mind if I have another piece of pie?"

"That's not possible," she blurted, the tears streaming again.

"Why? Do you have plans for the rest of this pie?"

"No, eat as much pie as you want. But I can't have children; I'm sterile." She was nearly sobbing now.

"Whoa, Samantha; you really need some whipped cream on this pie. It will cheer you up." He stood up. "Have you got any whipped cream in this fridge?"

"No, it's okay," she said, flapping her hand at him as he looked in the small, office-sized refrigerator. "I just got a little emotional seeing you again. I'll be fine."

"I am sure there is whipped cream somewhere on this campus. There's a huge fridge next door. I'll bet there's some in there." Before she could say another word he was through the door into Bunny's classroom. Just as quickly he came back, laughing in delight as he waved an aerosol can of whipped cream in the air. "They know how to live in there. They've got ice cream sandwiches in the freezer, six packs of sodas in the fridge, and bags of tortilla chips on the counter. I may have to befriend the teacher over there."

Samantha pulled her chin into her chest. "At your own risk," she said curtly.

He stood above her shaking up the can of whipped cream. "May I?" he asked politely.

She lifted her plate. "Please." He squirted a dollop of cream on the top of her half-eaten slice. She looked up at him, one eyebrow raised. "Kind of stingy—for a spiritual master and all."

"Well, Samantha, it's not really my whipped cream."

She smiled mischievously. "I would think whipped cream would be like the air—it's not like anybody could actually own it."

He shrugged. "Makes sense." He handed her the can. "Help yourself."

She squirted a generous portion of cream on her pie as he sliced another piece for himself. "Do you want more pie?" he asked her. "Anything else I can get you while I'm up?"

"No, I'm good."

"Of course you're good." He sat across from her again. "Where did you get the idea that you're sterile?" he asked gently, looking into her eyes.

"I guess it was all those failed fertility treatments," she said, finding it hard to hide a trace of bitterness in her voice.

"Doctors—particularly western doctors—they often can't see the big picture," he said nonchalantly. "Don't accept the limitations they try to put on you."

She smiled at him, determined to change the subject. "I'm so happy you're here, and this pie is amazing! What a great day."

"Exactly," Craig agreed.

Watching him take a hefty bite of pie, she wondered at where he had been, what he'd been doing in the decade since she'd last seen him. But at that moment she realized that she didn't wonder at the veracity of his spiritual claims. There was a calmness about his manner, a teasing playfulness in his voice that somehow conveyed authenticity to her.

"So what story are you going to tell me first?" he asked. "Why the pie lady is driving you crazy or why you think you're sterile?"

"First tell me about you," she said. "What have *you* been doing?"

"Doing," he repeated with a smirk. "Well I've never really done much of anything! It's never about doing, Samantha," he said, switching to a professorial tone. "It's about being."

She rolled her eyes. "Oh, c'mon," she persisted, adopting a teasing tone of her own. "Back when we first met you seemed to be 'doing' all the time! You were teaching Tae Kwon Do, and then hanging with your students at that pizza parlor you used to tell me about. Of course you had your daughters to take care of, re-landscaping your parents' yard--"

"You're right," he interrupted, conceding to her list. "We met right after my divorce, didn't we?"

"You told me it had been about a year."

He nodded silently, staring into the space above Samantha's head as if expecting an image to appear on the back wall. "I remember now." He smiled wryly then shook his head. "I've always been a homebody, you know, an introvert. I'm much more comfortable at home with my parents and my daughters, or just sitting alone meditating or reading a book, but that year—the year you caught me—well, I was out and about. Craig as social butterfly."

"Your public ministry?"

He nearly barked in surprise, his laughter so explosive at her comment. "I'm no preacher, Samantha. That's not my way. Though it's true when I was teaching at the dojo I had a lot of students who were interested in what I had to share." He took another bite and chewed carefully. "That time in my life was an anomaly."

"And now?" she asked cautiously.

"Well, now I'm once again leading a very quiet life."

"So," she continued, "no more late nights at the pizza parlor?"

"No late nights anywhere! I gave up the dojo and the pizza place."

"Oh, you don't teach anymore?"

"I only did that for a few years," he told her.

Samantha took another bite of pie, wondering how a spiritual master might prove his mastery without pupils to enlighten.

"You know," he said, his voice suddenly loud, "a master doesn't need to use words to convey knowledge. I can sit in the corner and chant, and the information you need will come to you."

She stared at him, aware that he had just read her mind or somehow intuited her thoughts. "I don't doubt that you could do that," she said softly. "But I like *talking* with you."

He smiled down at the last bits of pie on his plate and Samantha was surprised to see he looked humbled. "I like talking to you too." He finally looked up and she gazed into his pale blue eyes. She took a deep breath.

"So why did we stop talking?" she asked. "I needed you but you didn't return my calls."

"You *thought* you needed me," he corrected. "But you see, you didn't need me. In fact, our separation was necessary. You never would have been able to accomplish the work you came to do if I had been in close proximity. The energy that I was conducting and directing would have interfered with the energy you needed to direct. But with me out of the way, you were able to become a clear channel, and that's why you were able to accomplish so much."

"But I didn't accomplish anything! I failed."

"Samantha!" he said, laughing, "You didn't fail. Why would you think that you had failed?"

"Because the kids stop typing with me. They refused to type with me. And facilitated communication was dismissed as a hoax! If I hadn't failed, children with disabilities all over the world would have learned to facilitate, and they would be much more respected and honored—but I didn't do this job you told me I was supposed to do—and that didn't happen."

"Oh, Samantha—no, that's not true," he assured her. "You had a very specific job you had to complete. You were writing something very specific with the children at that time. It's as if you were drawing an energetic blueprint for ascension. That's what you were doing with those kids."

She shook her head, not believing him. "I stopped facilitating with them and nobody cared. Nobody wanted to believe it."

"Samantha, trust me: that was a very special group of children," he interjected.

"Well, of course they were special," Samantha agreed quickly. "That was the first class that was mine, my first class as a teacher. I loved those kids. Maybe I just wanted that for them so badly that I created the whole thing in my head."

"Samantha," he began again but she interrupted him.

"When they stopped typing with me—well, when they stopped typing things that made sense—a lot of them would only type one word: 'nom.' Over and over again. That was the beginning of that chant you taught me." She looked up at him. "Remember?"

"Of course," he agreed. "Nom meoho renge keo."

"You taught me that. They couldn't have known it. I had to have been guiding their hands."

Craig laughed gleefully. "Do you remember what 'nom' means, Samantha?"

She shook her head.

He lifted his hands seemingly delighted to impart fresh information. "Nom: it means devotion. Don't you see? They were expressing their devotion to you!"

She stared at him doubtfully for a moment. He nodded eagerly. "It's true, I'm sure of it!" Then he paused. "Unless they were trying to type the entire chant—nom meoho renge keo. You know what that means, don't you?"

"Something about the Lotus Sutra?" she said tentatively.

"Exactly! The Lotus Sutra. I'm no Buddhist scholar, but my understanding is that the Lotus Sutra is somewhat like a promise to delay enlightenment until all the other sentient beings are ready to join us."

Samantha rolled her eyes. "That'll take a good long time."

He laughed again. "Or it will happen instantly. Because how many sentient beings are there in reality?" He lifted his index finger. "There is only one consciousness. We are all one in the universal love energy, God consciousness."

Samantha smiled and turned her attention back to her pie. "I always loved your stories, Craig."

"Samantha!" he exclaimed. "You know this is more than a story. You know I'm telling you truth."

Samantha sighed as she lifted the last bite of pie to her mouth. "I guess I just don't understand."

"You don't have to understand, Samantha," he said. "Just know that you were the lead guide on that project. You weren't just facilitating with those kids, you were guiding them both physically and spiritually; you were like a weaver knitting all the threads of the story together. That was your role. And you succeeded. On the astral planes, you are highly honored for your role in the Facilitation project."

She stared at him in disbelief. "I don't know what you're talking about, but I feel so relieved." Her voice cracked and she dropped her gaze, hoping she wouldn't tear up again.

"Oh, Samantha." He sighed. "Do you want some more pie?"

"No."

"Can I have some more pie?"

"Sure," she whispered. "Go ahead."

He crossed the room with his empty plate and returned with it filled again. "No whipped cream?" she asked.

"Too much cholesterol." He grabbed another napkin off the table. "What surprises me, Samantha," he continued, "is that after completing a project like that, you still stuck around."

"Well, I hadn't intended to stick around," she said, dabbing her eyes with a Kleenex. "I got married and I moved to the foothills for a few years. But that didn't work out too well, so here I am again, back in the valley, back in the classroom."

"That's interesting," he said shortly, his gaze focused on his pie. "But I don't mean it's surprising that you're still teaching. I mean it's surprising that you're still in a body."

"What?" She pushed back her chair. "You mean you're surprised I'm still alive? You expected me to be dead by now?"

He swallowed, and lifted another forkful to his lips. "Samantha, you just don't appreciate the magnitude of the work you completed here. Spiritually, it was huge. For most people, that would be enough for one lifetime. But not you! I don't know what you're hanging around for, but I guess you've still got some big plans. Can't imagine what they might be!"

She snorted, expressing a mixture of humor and derision. "Hey, you and me both," she said. Craig gave her a questioning look, and she threw up her hands. "I don't know what I'm doing," she exclaimed. "I look at my life and I wonder: did I ever have goals? Did I ever have plans and dreams—or have I been drifting like this for decades? I had a profession, a career, a job I was good at—so when the marriage fell flat I came back to the classroom. But it doesn't feel like enough anymore."

"Samantha," he said gently. "You most certainly have set goals for yourself—I can assure you of that. Important tasks that you need and want to accomplish. You decided all this before you were born."

"Let me get this straight," she said, unable to hide a sarcastic tone. "Between lifetimes, I'm unselfish and altruistic, pledging to channel all this energy for the greater good. But then I get here and I'm whiny because I can't find a man and all that happ'ly-ever-after romantic crap!"

Craig laughed. "Listen, Samantha, I can't guarantee you the romantic crap you claim you want. But you have not given up your ticket to happiness. You can do whatever you want to do and still direct the energy you need to channel!"

She stared down at her hands, nodding and pressing her lips together. "All I really wanted to do," she whispered, "was to have a baby."

"Oh, well!" He paused to take a last bite of pie before answering. "Well, that's going to happen. Don't listen to those doctors, Samantha, because you're pregnant right now."

Samantha felt like her eyes were going to pop out of her head. "What?"

"You heard me. You're pregnant. No joke."

"But Craig," she said, "I already told you my ex-husband and I had all kinds of fertility treatments, and it's just not going to happen." She began to feel silly, her voice high-pitched and frantic. She cleared her throat, and deepened her register. "It's not going to happen," she repeated. "I need to accept that."

He nodded nonchalantly, seeming uninterested in her protests. "So your husband is completely out of the picture?"

"Right."

"Well," he said stretching, fork still in hand, "I know this isn't going to be an immaculate conception, so if there's no guy in the picture, maybe you're not pregnant yet. But if you're not yet, you will be soon."

She sat stunned, staring at him, feeling as if the floor was going to come up and meet her face any minute. She put her head down on the table,

"Do you want some water?" he asked. "I'll get you some water."

She heard him shuffling through the cupboards, then he strode to her side with a coffee mug filled with cold tap water. She lifted her head and sipped it slowly.

"So there is a guy, huh?"

"Uh huh."

"And it's not your ex-husband?"

"No."

He nodded slowly, sitting in the chair beside her. "There's more than one guy, isn't there?"

She jerked her head up. "Shut up! Jeez, how do you do that?'

He shook his head, finally having the grace to look a little embarrassed. "The information just comes to me, Samantha. I only know because you want me to know. If you hadn't wanted me to know you wouldn't have let me access that information."

"Are you sure—I mean, Tom and I tried for three years—and now—gee, I only--" She took a deep breath, gazing at his stoic expression. "Never mind," she said.

"I could be wrong," Craig conceded. "Wouldn't be the first time. Buy yourself a pregnancy test on the way home, Samantha. Then you'll know for sure."

"Maybe," she said slowly. "I'm not sure I want to know for sure."

He shrugged. "Up to you." He stood up slowly. "So will there be pie again tomorrow?"

"I don't know!" Samantha said chuckling a bit. "They show up when I least expect them."

He grinned, smugly lifting his eyebrows. "Kind of like the Craig vehicle."

She released a deep cleansing breath. "The Craig vehicle," she repeated affectionately.

He nodded. "It's best not to identify with the vehicle, Samantha. Identify with God essence. That's what we are. That's *who* we are."

"Okay," she said automatically, then she realized she wasn't sure what he had said. She felt as if her ears were plugged and her mind was racing. She laid her hand on her abdomen.

She felt Craig lean toward her. "It's going to be okay, Samantha. It's a new adventure, and there's purpose in it."

She looked up and caught him staring at her belly. She lifted her hand to push hair away from her face, and his gaze followed. "Are you going to be here again tomorrow?" she asked.

"Yes." He stood up. "They tell me they need me here for at least a week." He turned and headed toward the wastebasket at her desk. "I suspect I'll be here for the rest of the school year."

"Really—you think the regular guy will be out that long?"

He turned to squint and stare above her head. "I don't get any read on the guy who holds the permanent job here. I just see myself here as your pregnancy progresses. Probably May or June, don't you think?"

"Oh my God, Craig, this can't really be happening, can it? I never wanted to be a single mother."

"Look, don't worry about that. Trust that the universe is protecting you, okay?"

She exhaled audibly. "I'm going to go home now."

CHAPTER FOURTEEN

Samantha was swimming through salty water. It felt good, like being scrubbed with a rough brush. The smell of the ocean was clean and crisp. She breathed deeply, allowing the water to rush in and clean out her sinuses. Then she blew the water up high into the air. She turned in the water, feeling her legs pressed tight together, spinning like a corkscrew. She felt an urge to leap, and she let the impulse carry her up out of the water. She crashed into the waves—what a rush! The sun sparkled on the water like diamonds. She tried to stretch her arms up above her head, then realized she had no arms. She tried to bend her neck to get a better look at her body, but she had no neck. Her tiny eyes shifted left, right, up, down. It was impossible to get a good look at her body, at her vehicle. She shivered in the cold water, and oh, it felt so good. Ah, yes, I understand now, she thought. I am a whale.

The joyous realization of her true nature led her to leap into the air. Then she saw him—the yellow-billed magpie. His wings were fluttering unlike any other normal magpie's wings. He was hovering like a humming bird above the lapping water; he was waiting for her. The he darted away, speeding across the surface of the ocean, and she knew she had to follow. She knew she belonged with the magpie.

***

Late afternoon, Samantha put on an episode of *Bill Nye, The Science Guy* for the kids so she could sit in the back of the room and type with Lulu. It was hard to find time to do this with her. Bill Nye was talking to a cool scientist guy who worked with reptiles. The man was cradling a little tiny crocodile about the size of a Barbie doll with a tail. Lulu was rocking.

Anna had dutifully dug up two electric typewriters, Samantha didn't know where. She and Samantha exchanged a daily notebook chronicling their efforts. So far, it had not been completely futile, but there had been nothing that could verify that the words were coming from Luisa. Samantha read her stories—like chapters from the 4th grade textbook on California history—and then asked her comprehension questions. She generally answered correctly. Anna watched PBS with Luisa and asked her what her favorite TV shows were. Luisa surprised her mother by saying she didn't like cartoons, but enjoyed the news shows she could hear Anna listening to when she was working with Jessica in the other room. She told Samantha she liked her "Lulu" nickname. She told Anna she preferred Luisa.

Anna remained optimistic. "So she likes you to call her by the nickname you gave her, but she likes me to call her by the name I gave her," she noted insistently at her latest meeting with Samantha. "I don't see any inconsistency there. In fact I think she has great diplomacy!"

Samantha had smiled. She really wanted it to be true too. In fact, she believed it was true. She couldn't help it. "Oh, Anna, I do believe that she is communicating with us," she finally said aloud. "And yet, you know this isn't enough. I can come up with logical reasons to explain inconsistencies too. But still we need proof, before we can test where she is academically, before we can start fading the support out. We need some kind of proof."

"What will it take to convince you?" Anna challenged.

"Well, you know—we talked about this before--" Samantha began.

"I know; you want some kind of statement that one of us knows is true that the other one doesn't know. But that's up to Luisa, isn't it? It's up to her to decide if she wants us to know for sure."

"Do you think she's playing us?" Samantha asked, surprised.

"No, nothing like that," Anna said quickly. "But somehow, I don't know, I'm not sure how to put it--"

"She's testing us."

"Yes, exactly!" Anna agreed. "She wants to know our level of commitment to her."

"I can see that," Samantha said tersely.

"What?" Anna asked.

"Nothing."

Anna raised her eyebrows and stared at Samantha. "What?" she said again.

Samantha shook her head. "I don't know; we're both just guessing."

"So go ahead."

"No, I was just going to say that she maybe testing our level of commitment to each other as well."

Anna looked surprised. "Interesting."

Samantha shrugged. "I'm just speculating."

"Good," she said. "I like it when my people stick their necks out and say whatever may be on their minds. Thanks for taking the risk."

Samantha had nodded, but she felt uncomfortable. *Now I'm one of your people?* she had wondered to herself.

She thought of this as she held Lulu's hand. "Science rules," the TV said.

"Do you like Bill Nye?" Samantha asked Lulu.

"Yes," she typed. "He's very smart."

Samantha stifled a yawn. She'd been attempting facilitation with Lulu for over a month, and this was the kind of banal responses the girl had been giving her. "Lulu!" she exclaimed in a loud voice. "I can't believe that after all these years of silence, you sound like middle management. It sounds like you're saying what you think I want to hear. Nobody likes Bill Nye because he's smart. We like him because he's hilarious." She sat back for a moment, feeling a little guilty for snapping at the girl. "I'm sorry, sweetie; I just want you to know that you can be who you are. You can be yourself. Of course, maybe you don't know who that is yet. But it's okay to explore; it's okay to be creative."

She looked up and realized every set of eyes in the room was staring at her. "Sorry; I didn't realize I was so loud. Go back to Bill Nye. I'll quiet down back here." She felt her face burning. Maybe she was nuts. Maybe facilitated communication was just a big crazy hoax and she was as big a skeptic as everyone else. In fact she was the biggest skeptic of all. That's why it no longer worked, because she no longer believed. It was as if she had stopped believing in fairies and Tinker Bell had died.

Just then the back door swung open and Craig stuck his head inside. "Hey," he said in a soft voice. "Sorry; I'm kind of early. If you don't mind I'll just leave the cart in here, and then come back a little later—say 20 minutes?"

"Sounds good."

"Later, gator," he said with a grin.

"After a while, crocodile," she whispered.

As the door drifted closed, Lulu grabbed Samantha's hand. Samantha was surprised; it was the first time Luisa had initiated facilitation. Her hand darted toward the keys as if it were a small animal apart from the rest of her body, and certainly not under the control of Samantha. "That was him!" she typed frantically.

"That was who?" Samantha asked.

"That man," Lulu typed. "The man who came in and talked to you just now. He's the magpie. I've been looking for him. I see him in my dreams."

***

Samantha sat alone, cross-legged on the floor of the school library, leafing through a field guide to birds of Western North America. She stared at the familiar profile of magpies on page 327. There were two: the black-billed—which ranged through western Canada down through the western to central United States-- and the yellow-billed—almost never recorded outside the central valley of California. Virtually identical except for the yellow bill and a bit of yellow skin under the eye.

She propped the book open on the floor so she could gaze at the drawing as she searched the shelves for more books. The selection in an elementary school library was obviously slim. She'd do better to go to Amazon and take a quick cyber tour of bird books. She fingered each book quickly as she picked through the shelves. "Hello!" she said aloud. "What's this?" She pulled a picture book called "Bird Lore" from the shelf.

"Samantha?"

She jumped when she heard her name. "You startled me," she said, looking up to find Craig coming around the stacks. "Why are you looking for me?"

"I could hear you calling me!" he exclaimed. "You sounded kind of panicky."

She looked up at him in confusion, suddenly feeling very tired. "Panicky?"

"Well, you don't look panicky," he admitted. "Though you do look intense. What are you doing in here?" He twisted his head to get a look at the book open on the floor. "Bird watching?" he asked.

"Magpies," she said, lifting the book she held in her hand. She paused, gauging his reaction, but his face looked blank. "What do you think of magpies?"

He laughed. "Can't say I think about them all that much," he said. "They're the big black and white ones, right?"

She picked up the field guide and held it up for him to see. "Pretty birds," she said. "Not quite as big as crows but close."

"Why the sudden interest in magpies?" he asked.

"Don't you know?" she blurted. "Why don't you know?"

He narrowed his eyes and smirked at her. "I could guess why you're interested in magpies, and eventually I'd guess right—because I'm good at that—but it would be faster if you'd just tell me."

She stood up and faced him squarely, though she was way below his eye level. "You're the magpie!" she exclaimed emphatically. "I've been having this recurring dream for months, maybe even a year—yes, I think it's been at least a year—and in every dream there's a magpie, leading me somewhere, beckoning me."

Craig grinned. "And I'm the magpie?"

"Lulu told me that," she said. "When Lulu saw you, she suddenly had something to say. She grabbed my hand and started to type. She said: 'He's the magpie; I see him in my dreams.' But those are my dreams too. I don't know what it means."

Craig took the guide from her hand and sank into a chair. "This one with the yellow bill apparently stays here in northern California. I guess when you see a yellow-billed magpie in your dreams, that's a clear message to come here."

"Look—I just found this entry on magpies," she said holding up the picture book. "It says the magpie was the only bird that refused to come into Noah's ark. It stood on the roof through all that rain." She looked up at him. "So apparently that means that a magpie at your house is good luck, because it shows that the construction is sturdy and the roof will hold!"

"That's reassuring," Craig said, touching the page to get a better look at the blue and yellow illustration.

She sat down beside him at the table. "So do you feel like a magpie?"

"I don't think so," he said, laughing.

"Maybe I was guiding her hand," Samantha fretted. "I mean that's my dream, not hers. Of course, I certainly wasn't thinking about it this afternoon when I was typing with Lulu. But it's possible—I could have guided her hand. That's one explanation."

"The other explanation," Craig said in an emphatic, nearly annoyed voice, "is that you and Lulu shared a series of recurring dreams, and it's not a coincidence that the two of you were brought together like this. Samantha, that should be obvious."

"Nothing is obvious, Craig," she said, her voice sounding frantic. "I can't presume that this is some sort of fanciful adventure this time. I can't presume that this child is some kind of wunderkind who will change the world. I need some kind of proof, some kind of verifiable evidence that shows she's intelligent and capable of sophisticated conversation. And then we can get an accurate academic assessment completed and be better able to determine her needs—how to assist her to progress academically and socially. That's my job, that's what I get paid to do. I don't get paid to write the next book of the Bible, or some kind of fanciful new age message for the masses. That's not my job."

She looked for Craig's reaction, but he seemed serenely undisturbed by her tirade. Without a word or glance, he jumped up and walked directly to a bookshelf on the other side of the room. He pulled out a book. "Check this out," he said, strolling back to her. "Look—'Avian Tales.'" He flipped to a page in the center of the book and began to read aloud. "'Magpies are kin to crows.' Oh, and listen to this: 'The magpie is the most intelligent member of the Corvid family.' He grinned and nodded. "Yeah, that's what I'm talking about. I could be a magpie. I'm smarter than your average bear, right?"

"How did you find that book?" she asked, astonished.

"I listened carefully and it called me over."

"Seriously?" she asked a trace of incredulity in her voice.

"Seriously," he confirmed without irony. "That's how I found you this afternoon too. I could hear you calling—with your heart. You were in here, but you really wanted to talk to me. You were very loud and insistent. It would have been impossible to ignore you."

"And the book?" she asked. "Was it loud and insistent too?"

"No, I was the one calling out to the book," he said with a shrug. "I just asked if there was something else I needed to know, and I was directed to this book."

She leaned back, feeling amazed, but she decided to adopt the nonchalant façade he seemed to exhibit. "So," she said, "what else does the book say?"

He studied the page. "It says that magpies are scavengers and thieves and they especially like to grab shiny objects." He grimaced in mock horror. "Well, that's embarrassing," he said.

She laughed. "Not so pretty now, huh?"

"'This reputation for stealing indicates a great talent for using whatever they happen to find. In other words the magpie is adept at making do with the tools available.' That makes sense."

"Does it?" Samantha asked sincerely. "You identify with that?"

He lowered his eyebrows as if to better focus on the problem at hand. "I feel, Samantha, as if the author here is describing all of us of master status who are in human form. We have to make do. Would it be easier to drop our bodies and deal with pure energy? Of course. But we cobble together what we need because of and in spite of the limitations imposed by this flesh--because this is the adventure we have chosen! And it's the human body that makes it both possible and necessary!"

"What do you mean?"

"Like magpies, we have used what we had on hand—the human DNA—to create God consciousness. Our DNA is our magnetic connection to the Divine. It's a beautiful crystal that vibrates in every cell—and it's God in every atom of our body. It's amazing isn't it?"

She smiled at him. "Does the book say anything else?"

"It says magpies make big messy nests that look like balls of sticks, but actually they're gateways to an underworld where spiritual knowledge may be gained. Isn't that great?"

She gave him a weak smile, then rested her chin in her hands. "I don't know, Craig. I'm not sure what any of it means. Why would Lulu be dreaming about you? Or magpies?"

"Well," Craig said slowly as he closed the book. "If I had a dream or a vision about a yellow-billed magpie, I'd certainly think about coming to California to find that bird. Maybe that's what Lulu did."

***

The road ahead was shaded with cypress trees, their stiff hair swept back away from the ocean. Samantha walked slowly, listening to the crunch of pine needles under her feet. Her face was hot and she liked the feeling of sea spray against her cheeks. It seemed she was walking through a tunnel, but she could see the sun shining at the end. She came out at the edge of a rugged cliff, the ocean a cobalt blue below her, the bark of sea lions calling her from a rock in a small cove. Then he was there, the yellow-billed magpie, cawing like a crow, beckoning her to take off, to fly with him, to launch herself off the cliff and upward into the air, or downward to the rocks. Without thinking she ran toward him, going faster and faster in an orgasmic rush into the sky, and she was flying too. She was a magpie just like Craig. Now she needed to go home, home to the valley.

CHAPTER FIFTEEN

Samantha was awakened by a ringing phone. She glanced at the yellow light of the digital clock radio as she forced herself to pull on the lamp light. 4:33. "Hello?" she said hoarsely.

"Sam! Oh my God, I forgot about the time difference! I woke you up, didn't I?"

It was Charlie. She wanted to berate him for waking her; she wanted to chew him out for not calling for so long. "Where are you?" she asked harshly.

"New Haven, at my Mom's house. Well, I just got back here. I've been at the hospital most of the night with her. I flew back here last month when my sister called to tell me about my mother's first stroke. She was doing pretty well, walking with a walker and all, but last night she had a second stroke. This doesn't look good at all."

"I'm sorry," Samantha said.

"Yep." There was silence on the other end, and Samantha wondered if he was crying. She felt a great burning in her chest, wanting to blurt out something, she wasn't sure what. She bit her upper lip hard, hoping to quell any desire to say that she missed him, that she wanted to see him again, and certainly she would not reveal any suspicions she had that she might be pregnant. She still didn't know for sure, and it wouldn't be appropriate to saddle him with that when his mother was dying.

"So how are you, O'Malley?" he said with forced cheeriness. "I've missed you."

She was startled by this, and suddenly angry. *Doesn't seem like you missed me!* She wanted to scream, but she wasn't ready to tip her hand. She swallowed hard. "I'm good," she squeaked. "Work is good. The weather is good here. I've been doing some gardening."

"Great! What did you plant?"

"Roses," she said. "I planted two rose bushes—a yellow one and a red one. And an orange tree—mandarin oranges."

"Sounds nice."

"How are you?" she asked. "Are you doing okay?"

"Well, it's not easy, of course. But I'm okay, I'm dealing."

"That's good," she said, stifling a yawn. "Umm--" She paused, unwilling to reveal any desire.

"What? Did you say something?"

"I just, uh, I was just wondering if you're coming back, you know, anytime soon."

"Well, it's hard to say. I don't know what's going to happen here. I've always thought that someday I'd move back east again. Dale's a senior now. I have to admit I've been thinking about it. This might be the right time, you know, what with my Mom's health, and all—or if—well, I can't think about it right now." He coughed. "Look, I just wanted to hear your voice, that's all. I wanted to tell you how happy I am we reconnected—you know, even if it was just for one night."

Adrenaline shot from her chest to her eyelids. "Are you saying goodbye?" she exclaimed. "Is that why you called?"

"No! I told you, I called because I wanted to hear your voice. I wish I could be with you. Don't you think I'd rather be with you right now?"

"I'm sorry," she said quickly, remembering how he used to complain sometimes that she was needy, that she liked to stay home too much, that she had gotten too dependent on him. "I'm still half asleep you know," she shot in a disclaimer.

"Is something wrong? Are you okay?"

"It's all fine, Charlie. I can handle it."

"Handle what, Sam? Is something going on?"

"No!" she proclaimed frantically. "Everything is fine. Don't worry about me."

"I wasn't worrying. You're a strong woman, Ms Omm. You're an oak. No wind is going to knock you down."

"I'd rather be a redwood," she said slyly.

"Sorry; I forgot what a loyal Californian you are. That only makes sense. Look, I'll call again when I get a chance."

"You don't have to," she said. "I'm fine."

"Is something wrong, Samantha? Do you not want me to call?"

"No, you can call," she said hastily. "I want you to call. But not on my account, you know. I'm okay."

"Whatever, Sam," he said, not hiding his annoyance.

"Charlie, wait; don't hang up."

"What?"

"I'm sorry; I'm just sleepy, you know." She felt herself choking up. "I've been, um, preoccupied, you know. I care about you. I want you to keep me posted about your Mom, and about how you're doing. So please call, I want you to call."

"When I can, Sam. You know, just to hear your voice."

***

Unable to get back to sleep after Charlie's call, Samantha got up and dressed, ate a bland breakfast of soda crackers and a hardboiled egg, then got to the classroom early. The morning nausea was continuing and she knew that soon it would be impossible to ignore Craig's pronouncement that she might be pregnant. She drank a cup of weak coffee with milk just before the kids arrived. She still felt sick to her stomach, but at least she was alert.

At recess she sat at her desk, alone in the room, nibbling on graham crackers she kept on hand for the kids. Jumpy and agitated, she stared at the shifting colors of her computer screen saver, too distracted to read emails. *Don't think about it, don't think about it,* she chanted silently even as she stared down at her belly and breasts. Was she getting bigger or not? And what if she was pregnant? Would she be happy, scared, embarrassed? In need of financial advice, psychological support, new clothes, hemorrhoid cream? "Don't think about it," she said aloud. But certainly today, yes today, she must stop and buy a pregnancy test on the way home. *It'll be negative,* she scolded herself, *and then you'll be disappointed.*

She didn't rise when the bell rang. The nausea had faded, but she was left with a strange twinge on her lower left side. She took a deep breath and clicked on the cheery newsletter sent out weekly from the new principal. Jenna Finch was young, mid 30s, Samantha guessed, and she was pretty, slim and blond. So why did she choose to dress like Miss Piggy? Flippy shoulder length hair, big sweeping skirts and blouses with ruffles. Jenna was way too young for a Mother Goose-y look, so what was the point? Samantha had become accustomed to the severe style of ambitious young female administrators: boyish haircuts, dark tailored suits and patent leather pumps. That was too extreme for Samantha's taste as well, but Jenna's flowery fashion left Samantha wondering if the new principal had the strength to discipline the rowdier members of the student body—and of the faculty.

Saving the newsletter to read later, Samantha clicked to close the computer screen. She glanced at the clock. Seven minutes had passed since the bell had rung: where were the kids? Rose and Valerie were a Godsend, daily escorting the class to and from recess and lunch, but where were they now? She urged her aides to keep cell phones in their pockets so they could call her when needed. She pulled her own phone out as she stood and headed for the door. No missed messages. "I'm sure everything is fine," she muttered to convince herself.

The soothing, melodic rumble and squeal of children's voices flowed toward Samantha as she moved down the hall. She rounded the corner to see Rose holding Lulu's hand, standing sentry over a bench of seated children. Samantha counted as she walked closer: someone was missing and of course it was Echo.

"Echo is missing," "Valerie is looking for her," several voices announced in staccato patter. A torrent of question followed. "Can't we all go look for her?" "Can't we all go inside?" "Did you bring us a snack?"

"Don't you have your cell phone?" Samantha pointedly asked Rose.

"Yes, yes," the assistant admitted. "I should have called you." But Samantha had no time for discussion. "Call the office; tell them how long Echo's been missing. Tell them she has no documented history of running off campus, but there's no telling what a child like Echo will do. Take the rest of the kids to play on the jungle gym. I'm going to search."

She took off at a jog, wondering if she should head toward the park at the far end of the playground. Echo could have easily left campus that way. But first she needed to explore the nooks and crannies around the school: the bathrooms, any empty offices, narrow corridors between trailers and portable buildings. She wanted to find Valerie so they could coordinate their efforts, but her gut told her to keep moving.

She ran into a girls' bathroom, dutifully checked in each stall, darted through the gate at the bus stop and then headed toward the cafeteria.

Through the open doors she could hear a cacophony of keening wails and sharp retorts. She slowed down and entered cautiously.

A kindergarten class was moving through the lunch line. Teacher and aides hovered protectively, directing the students through a side door, herding them back toward the classroom rather than to their usual table. Bunny's class was already seated. Her two assistants lifted their heads like border collies sniffing the wind when they saw Samantha enter the cavernous room. They glared at her, then pointed with chins and chests to a corner in the back where a knot of people formed a pulsing cluster of screams and shouts. Two custodians, three lunch ladies, a noon-duty supervisor, and the usual half dozen parents who seemed to have nothing better to do than to hang at the school all morning gathered in a vibrating semi-circle, their attention directed to the floor. For five seconds or less, Samantha was frozen by the sight, but then a voice rang out above the rest. "Ms O'Malley!" Valerie cried. "Come quickly! Please!"

The crowd parted and Samantha could see Echo screaming and writhing on the floor while Bunny held her down in an old fashioned one-person restraint. Bunny sat behind Echo, her legs straddling Echo's legs, her arms holding Echo's arms. Bunny was a large woman, but tiny Echo was giving her a run for her money. Samantha noted that Bunny's ropey muscles bulged as she held onto the desperate child.

Valerie knelt at Echo's feet stroking her legs with firm pressure, talking softly, trying to sooth her. "Calm down, sweetie. Please, Echo, calm down."

But Echo would not calm down. She thrashed and thrashed. She leaned toward Bunny's arm, her mouth open, trying to bite her. Frustrated at that attempt, she flung her head back, trying to hit Bunny's face with the back of her skull. She paused to wail, tears streaming, breath panting. Then her thrashing began again.

Samantha was horrified at the spectacle. The twinge on her left side throbbed harder and her face was hot. *How dare you* were the words that bubbled at her lips, but she swallowed hard to keep them in her mouth. She moved closer as if pulled by an invisible string. Echo saw her and cried out. "Ms O'Malley! Make her stop!"

Bunny looked up at Samantha and her taut face registered a mix of satisfaction and disdain. "This filly needs to be broken!" she snorted with a humorless chuckle. Then to Echo: "Do you hear me, missy? I will break you. I am much stronger than you are. I could do this all day."

Samantha felt like an impotent fool, standing there, separate from this mad display. She realized both Echo and Bunny needed a strong dose of Skinnerian behavior modification, but she felt inadequate to the task. Kindergarteners were being escorted out, but more classes were entering. Echo, young, wild, and stoked on adrenaline, showed no sign of fatigue. All of Samantha's training had groomed her to avoid situations like this. But Bunny was bragging about endurance: might this hostage standoff go on for hours?

Unthinking, Samantha sunk to her knees next to Valerie at Echo's feet. She steadied herself on Valerie's gentle shoulder, the other on Echo's foot. "You need to calm down, Echo," Samantha said, well aware that her nasally plea sounded like a whine.

"Nooo!" Echo hollered, her voice deeper and louder than before, like an Irish Banshee come to portent a death.

"Stop it, you brat," Bunny yelled and Samantha felt her resolve.

"Echo," she said in a strong clear voice. "Promise me you will come take my hand when Mrs. Schwartz lets you go."

Bunny's head jerked up. She fastened a hostile gaze on Samantha's face. "I will let her go when she can be a good polite girl and not a minute sooner."

Samantha glanced away quickly, ignoring Bunny to look again at Echo. "Promise, Echo," she said firmly. "Promise me you will come to me."

Echo stopped yelling. "I promise."

Samantha leaned back and nodded at the girl. She stood up and looked down at Bunny. "Mrs. Schwartz," she said, "please let Echo go."

"No," Bunny said harshly. "Not until she apologizes."

Samantha took a deep breath, afraid she might roll her eyes at this new childish demand. She spoke slowly as if addressing one of her students. "We can work that out later, Mrs. Schwartz, but right now I need you to let Echo go."

Bunny grimaced and her nostrils flared. At that moment Samantha wouldn't have been surprised to see steam gushing out of Bunny's nose and ears. Still Samantha stood her ground, trying to soften her face, wanting to appear as a friendly colleague, rather than the angry combatant she truly was.

Bunny's compliance was sudden: she flung her arms and legs in the air, away from tiny Echo. "Fine," she blurted, a short resentful message. Then Echo was jumping to her feet, leaping into Samantha's arms, sobbing in a loud voice. Samantha looked down and patted the child on her back. She couldn't help but wonder if Echo wasn't being more than a little theatrical in her showy switch from anger to sorrow. But then, Samantha thought, who am I to judge? This girl was born in a hash oil lab and bounced from foster home to foster home. Was she re-living some horrid memory right then in the claw-like grip of Bunny Schwartz? Worse yet, might Echo be incapable of genuine emotion, but had learned to maneuver from one ordeal to the next by flashing extreme displays of defiance and drama whenever the situation seemed to call for it?

Valerie touched Echo with sympathy too, and yet she took the opportunity to lean close. "You see, Echo," she said. "That's what happens when you don't follow directions."

Samantha bit her lip, resisting an urge to ask what direction Echo had refused to follow. Right now it didn't matter. The restraint Bunny had been using was clearly illegal, but more than that it was ineffective. No matter what noncompliant behavior had sparked it, Bunny's actions most certainly escalated the situation. In Samantha's eyes, Bunny was a bully, and despite her boasted years of experience, she came across as a rank amateur.

Echo continued to sob, despite Samantha's whispered admonishments that she needed to quiet down and start walking back to the classroom.

Bunny brought herself slowly to her feet, her mouth puckered as if tasting something sour. She shook her head, staring at Samantha's face. "It's no wonder she's out of control," Bunny hissed. "The way you spoil her."

Valerie gasped at the cutting insult. Samantha felt slapped, but she'd been around the block enough times to know to keep her mouth shut. "Let's go, Echo," she murmured, and indeed it seemed Echo was ready to move. The tiny child spun around suddenly, took a step toward Bunny and spat full in the teacher's face. "You don't talk to my teacher that way!" Echo declared.

Everyone gasped this time, Samantha included. She grabbed and pulled Echo back, scared Bunny might lay hands on her again, perhaps attempt to strike her. But even Bunny stood stunned and gaping. It seemed a small bomb had just exploded and this shocked silence was seeping through the room like smoke.

"What is going on here?"

Samantha turned as the booming voice of Principal Jenna Finch shattered the quiet. Still griping Echo's shoulders, Samantha took a step back in awe of the amazing gravitas Jenna managed to convey, even in her frilly clothes and girlish hairdo. "Echo!" the principal addressed the child in a stern but non-accusatory way. "Ms Rose told me you were missing. We've all been very worried about you, Echo."

Echo gazed down at the floor, actually appearing contrite. "I'm sorry," she mumbled. Samantha's heart soared.

But Bunny broke in. "This child needs to be suspended, and if it were up to me, we'd schedule an expulsion hearing as well."

"No!" Echo squealed, taking on yet another dramatic persona, perhaps the damsel-in-distress, clutching her hands between chest and throat, looking like she might swoon.

Jenna assertively stepped forward. "Let's go to the office, Echo. Looks like we've got a lot to discuss."

"No!" Echo repeated, this time with a defiant angry inflection, and she jerked away from Samantha seeking escape. Jenna and Valerie blocked her.

Samantha embraced her again. "Could I take Echo to Mrs. West's office to calm down?" Samantha asked referencing the school counselor.

"Mrs. West isn't here today," Jenna reminded her.

"I know," Samantha said. "I just think it's a good close place to take Echo so she can calm down."

Bunny sneered. "Ms O'Malley has to take care of her pet."

Samantha felt a chill on the back of her neck but she stared straight ahead at the principal, refusing to respond to Bunny. "We need to get Echo calm before we can do anything else," Samantha whispered.

"That's what I was doing," Bunny exclaimed. "But it wasn't good enough for Ms O'Malley."

Samantha grit her teeth and shifted her gaze quickly between the principal and her angry colleague. She took a deep breath. Was this principal going to allow another teacher to taunt her like this in front of children, staff members and parents? She couldn't work like this. Would she need to go job-hunting again? Was her road narrowing before her, making only one choice possible?

"You'll come with me now, won't you, Echo?" Samantha asked.

"Not to the office!" Echo said frantically. "I don't want to go to the office!"

"You see!" Bunny crowed triumphantly. "You see how defiant this girl is!"

Jenna spun on her heel, her wide skirt flaring out. "Go to lunch, Mrs. Schwartz," she ordered in a curt tone. "Ms O'Malley and I will handle it from here."

Samantha exhaled with relief, and unable to escape a small amount of smugness, she turned to view Bunny's reaction to the principal's rebuff. But Bunny seemed not to notice or care. She smiled slyly, her eyes narrowed and creased as her gaze focused on Samantha's breasts and abdomen. Finally she lifted her eyes to Samantha's face and raised her eyebrows in a knowing glare. She cocked her chin in a haughty salute then turned and marched out of the cafeteria.

Realizing the implication of Bunny's gloating smile, Samantha felt ill, but she had no time for surprise or embarrassment. Jenna was leading them away to the counselor's office. Echo was eager to get inside and hunker down in the counselor's comfy beanbag chair. Leaving Valerie to babysit the volatile Echo, Jenna pulled Samantha outside the door. "So what happened?" she demanded abruptly.

Samantha licked her lips, wondering if Jenna had intended to sound accusatory or simply brusque. She lifted her shoulders and spoke in a deliberately even tone. "I don't know. I came into the cafeteria looking for Echo. Mrs. Schwartz had her on the floor in a one-person restraint. I--"

Jenna interrupted. "Is a restraint like that authorized in her Individual Education Plan?"

"No," Samantha replied, equally business-like. "No restraints are authorized in Echo's IEP. In fact, last I heard, restraints that can be administered by only one person have been deemed too dangerous and are no longer legal in California. Only two person restraints are legal and only in the case of an aggravated assault. Quite frankly, I don't think a child Echo's size is capable of what the law would call an aggravated assault—you know—unless she has a weapon of some kind. She's too small."

Jenna stared into space, her mouth pressed into a straight line and her eyes narrowed. "All right, I get it." She turned quickly to look at Samantha. "Look," she began in a loud angry tone, and Samantha took a step back. Jenna saw and understood. "I'm sorry," Jenna said, "I think we're all a little on edge right now." She paused to smile and comically shiver as if casting off layers of stress. She touched Samantha's arm. "I don't know what just happened but I will be interviewing every person in that room to find out. I want to keep an open mind, but I want you to know this: I don't like the way Mrs. Schwartz was talking to you in front of the kids. That's not okay and I will tell her so. If she's got a beef with you, fine, let's sit down and hash it out. But you don't do it in front of students." She exhaled, then stared expectantly at Samantha as if waiting for confirmation or confession. Samantha was dumbfounded but grateful. "Thank you," she blurted.

But Jenna seemed unsatisfied. "So?" she asked.

Samantha raised her eyebrows blankly.

"So," Jenna repeated. "Is there a problem between you and Bunny?"

Samantha shrugged, tempted to say more, but answering honestly. "Not that I'm aware of."

"Well," Jenna continued, "the two of you obviously have different styles."

Samantha nodded. "Very different."

"Mrs. West tells me I might want to sit outside Bunny's classroom someday and have a listen."

Samantha smiled. "You're welcome to come sit in my classroom. You can hear her fine from in there."

Jenna nodded. "I just might do that. But in the meantime, I do need to suspend Echo. Regardless of whether she was provoked, I saw her spit in a teacher's face."

Samantha nodded. "Agreed."

"So when she calms down, bring her to the office. I'll have Rebecca call her mother--"

"Jenna," Samantha said. "I don't know if I can get Echo to the office. It might set her off again."

"Sam, Echo needs to follow the rules like everyone else--"

"But Jenna, what is our goal here? You can suspend her whether she comes to the office or not. We want her to leave campus as quietly as possible. I'll call her mom, explain the situation and then we can meet right here in Cecelia's office. What does it matter?"

Jenna nodded, considering. "But Sam," she said, "if Echo's so out of control, how can we be sure her mom will be able to handle her?"

"Echo *wants* to be with Mom. She does not want to return to foster care."

"Oh!" Jenna shook her head slowly. "She was a foster kid. I get it now. Look, you call her mother. I'm going to go read her online file right now."

The two women set off in different directions. Samantha limped a little as the pain in her side seemed to drag her down. She stifled a yawn, knowing she would be working through her lunch break.

CHAPTER SIXTEEN

For the rest of the day Rose was left babysitting the class with a half dozen Reading Rainbow dvd's to entertain them. Valerie was sequestered with a subdued Echo and Samantha was rushing from meeting to meeting: first with Jenna, then with Echo's mom, and finally with the Special Ed Director who made a rare surprise appearance on campus. During free minutes she planted herself at the computer, typing furiously to file a required addendum to Echo's Behavior Support Plan.

At one point, Samantha passed Valerie in the main office as her aide was leaving Jenna's office. "Val," she said, "I need to know: what happened?"

Valerie leaned in to whisper. "I went into the cafeteria looking for Echo. She and Mrs. Schwartz were nose to nose in a big yelling match."

"Did Echo hit Bunny?"

"No, Echo was leaning forward, her hands in her back pockets. Bunny told her she was not supposed to be in the cafeteria at this time. She told her to leave. Echo laughed in her face and said, 'You can't make me!'"

Samantha drew in a sharp breath, feeling the pain in her side as she recalled how frustrated she herself felt when Echo said those exact words to her. "What did Bunny say?"

"She said, 'Watch me,' and then she grabbed Echo and took her down."

Samantha's mouth dropped open. "That's illegal, you know. It's illegal for any school personnel to touch a child except in self-defense or defending someone else –and even then, it's a very risky thing to do. None of us should ever—you know that, don't you?"

Valerie nodded. "I do know. But I didn't know how to stop her."

A few hours later, Samantha was happy to hear the bell ring, happy that they would have a few Echo-free days due to the girl's suspension, and happy that she could trust Rose and Valerie to walk the kids to the bus stop. She emailed her report to Jenna, to her program specialist and a few other select district personnel as she had been instructed to do. She hit "print" so she could keep a hard copy in her file. As the printer worked its magic, she rested her head on her arms, closing her eyes. Her left side felt on fire.

She heard the door swing wide. She opened an eye to see Craig enter the room. "What's the matter?" he asked.

She sat up reluctantly, propping her chin in her cupped hands. "This has been a monster day," she uttered. "I don't know how I've made it through feeling as lousy as I do." She leaned back, surprised to find him staring at her. His eyebrows were lowered in deep concentration, his arms were raised and his hands were cupped as if he was patting a bubble formed above her head.

She squinted, giving him a questioning look but he said nothing so she stood up slowly. "I'm going to go home and take a nap."

"I don't think so," Craig said. "I don't think you should be alone."

"I'm okay," she said. "Just a funny pain in my side. Probably some weird virus."

"No, Samantha," he said, opening the door to the hallway again. "I'm going to drop this in the storage room, and then I'm going to take you to the ER. This is serious."

"Why would I go to the ER? I don't feel that bad."

"Get your purse; we're leaving," he insisted. "You've got five minutes for me to get this stuff stowed, tell the office we're leaving, and then we're out of here."

"Wait a minute; I don't even know what hospital to go to."

He paused in the doorway. "Call your doctor; tell him to meet you at the hospital."

She stood frozen for a moment. He had always been a gentle guide, proffering advice, not commands. "I'll call the advice nurse," she said, bending to reach into a lower file cabinet drawer for her purse.

"Just make it fast," he said as he darted out the door.

Samantha found her insurance card in her wallet, sat down at her desk and dialed the number. The nurse asked her symptoms and Samantha described the pain in her side, how it had started out small and gotten more intense as the day went on. "Could you be pregnant?" the nurse asked.

Samantha licked her lips, "I don't think so."

"Well," the nurse said haughtily, "if you're sexually active, and you still have all your reproductive organs, then it's a possibility. It needs to be considered."

Samantha took a deep breath. "Okay."

"On a scale of one to ten, how great is your pain?" the nurse asked.

"I don't know. Maybe a six."

"I'm going to send you over to the urgent care center on Folsom Boulevard," the nurse decreed. "I'll tell them you're coming so they'll be expecting you."

The thought of a long wait at Urgent Care was more than Samantha could bear. "Umm, couldn't I just get some kind of prescription so I can go home?" she asked meekly. "I really feel like going home and going to bed. In fact, maybe I could get a prescription from a pharmacy that delivers. Do you think we could just do that?"

"You feel like going home to bed, but your pain is only a six?" the nurse asked skeptically. "Look, if you feel that bad, you need to go the emergency room. You need to go to the emergency room now. Can you do that? Can you get yourself there? Is there someone who can drive you? If not you've got to call 911, because you cannot go home and lie on the couch."

"Okay."

"No, you promise me: you're going to the ER, right?"

"Right, it's okay. A friend of mine is here; he'll drive me."

"Okay. Go to Mercy General Hospital. I'm going to tell them you're coming."

"Okay."

Craig dropped her at the door of the emergency room and went to park the car. She passed through a narrow hallway, walking slowly, clutching her side, looking for someone to notify, someone who would take notice of her, so she could find a chair and curl into a ball. She saw a line in front of a desk and she stood there, looking around, wondering if she was in the right line, if she had come to the right place.

The line had moved and it would be her turn next when Craig came up behind her. "Here," she heard him say.

She turned to look at him; he had pushed a wheel chair up behind her. "Sit down," he commanded.

She felt embarrassed that a big fuss was being made over her. She hated to appear needy. "Someone else must need that more than I do," she mumbled.

"Hey," he said with a sly grin, "I went to all the trouble of tipping over some poor paraplegic and dumping him on the floor, just so you could have this chair. Don't be ungrateful."

"That's not really funny," she said irritably.

"Just sit down."

She sat obediently as the person at the head of the line finished and moved aside. Craig pushed her to the counter. "Hi," she said. "I have this pain in my side and the advice nurse sent me here." She realized sadly that she sounded apologetic. She cleared her throat.

"She's said she'd tell you I was coming."

The woman behind the glass had a narrow face and the smallest nose Samantha had ever seen. Her voice was high pitched. "What's your name?"

"Samantha O'Malley."

She typed furiously into her computer, seeming to enter a lot more letters than those in Samantha's name. Samantha breathed shallowly, but vowed to be patient. She was nearly wincing with pain now. The receptionist nodded. "Address?" she asked.

Samantha swallowed hard. "Oh, um--" she took another deep breath, "my address is--"

Craig reached around her. "Here," he said. He had taken Samantha's driver's license from her wallet. "Here's all her information."

"Thank you," the receptionist said slowly. "Is this current?"

"Yes," Samantha confirmed. "I just got a new driver's license last month."

"Fine." She proceeded with her typing.

"And the pain is on your lower right side?"

"No, the left side," Samantha corrected. "It's on my left side."

"Could you be pregnant?"

"I don't know, but--"

"Yes," Craig interjected. "She's pregnant."

"Craig--"

"Are you Mr. O'Malley?" the receptionist asked. "Are you her husband?"

"No!" Craig said emphatically.

"But you're the father?"

"God, no!" he blurted. "The Craig vehicle is not going down that road again!"

"Excuse me?" the receptionist asked pointedly.

"I'm sorry, but I don't actually know for sure that I'm pregnant," Samantha said wearily. "Are we done yet?"

"Just a few more questions."

The pain in Samantha's abdomen suddenly became extremely intense. She doubled over involuntarily. "Oh, God help me," she exclaimed, as she rocked frantically in the chair. "Oh God."

"Just a few more questions, ma'am," the receptionist said sternly. "I'll try to be quick."

Samantha felt a sharp blade shooting into her belly, and she slid down out of the chair. "Ma'am!" she heard the receptionist squeal. "You need to be patient for a few more minutes." But Samantha couldn't move. She was in a dark place. She could hear the familiar buzz and hum of people's voices, the rush of electronic machinery rumbling, hissing all around her, and the voice of the receptionist over it all. "Ma'am! Please sit up, ma'am."

"Samantha," she heard Craig saying her name and she felt his hands on her shoulders. "Samantha." He paused. "She can't hear you," he said to the receptionist.

Samantha thought this was very funny. *No, Craig,* she wanted to say, *you're wrong!* Imagine that! Craig is wrong. That doesn't happen very often. But he is wrong because I *can* hear her; I just can't move. Maybe I've left my body. Maybe this is what it's like to die. But aren't I supposed to rise above my body? Aren't I supposed to go up and look at the whole room, see the efforts to revive me? Maybe they're not trying to revive me. Maybe they're just down there arguing about whether I can hear them or not. Where's the light? Isn't there supposed to be a light?

It was all so dark. Samantha moved through the blackness wishing she could extend her hands before her, a little worried that she might run into something, but she couldn't seem to find her hands. Still she moved, and there was nothing discernable, no room, no stars, no light. And yet she could sense movement. She was being pulled toward something, something purposeful. Finally she saw a bush, a huge six-foot tall rose bush with dark red flowers, but no leaves, just blossoms and thorns. In the center was a nest of straw and wattle, a large nest with a roof. Out of an impossibly small side entry popped a yellow-billed magpie, squawking and flapping his wings. He cocked his avian black head, diving straight down through the thorny branches of the rose bush, twisting like a ray of light rather than a bird made of feather and bone. Samantha followed. Without thought or intent, she progressed forward without moving her limbs or her head, pushing forward as if she were watching this adventure on a TV monitor. The bird led her down, down, diving at a rapid pace through the branches and knobby trunk of the bush into the roots, into the ground, into a subterranean tunnel. She followed without fear, without hesitation, even without curiosity. This was simply what there was to do. The bird darted and the world passed at a dizzying speed. Then before her she saw Lulu, laughing and running, tagging her and bidding her to chase her. Lulu held up a screen of some kind, a cell phone perhaps. "I am God essence," she typed. Then she held up the machine and the words appeared without Lulu having to type them; it seemed the machine was hooked right into Lulu's brain. "I have come to observe. I have come to prepare. You are leading me now, but someday I will lead you. Thank you for your servitude." She laughed and laughed. "Be happy, Samantha," she vocalized in a surprising low voice.

CHAPTER SEVENTEEN

Samantha opened her eyes, and heard Craig's voice at her ear. "Good move, Samantha," he whispered. "Way to get attention."

"What?" she said groggily. "Where are we?"

She was lying on a gurney surrounded by pulsing green curtains. Lights were yellow and bright, and for a split second Samantha suspected she had awakened inside a dome of molded green Jell-O. Everything was fluorescent. Everywhere there was movement. She was flanked by two blurry people in green, one at her right arm, one at her left. Craig was at her head speaking low into her ear. "You're in the emergency room, remember?" Craig said. "And you passed out. It was brilliant. Got you moved to the head of triage immediately."

"You awake?" the blurry figure at her left arm asked in a gentle masculine voice. He was inserting an IV needle into her vein. "The doctor has ordered an ultrasound," the blurry figure at her right informed her as she fastened a blood pressure cuff onto Samantha's other arm. "A technician will be here to take you down the hall to X-ray in a few minutes."

The two figures in green scrubs vibrated beyond the curtains and were gone. Samantha struggled to turn her head toward Craig. "How long was I unconscious?" she asked.

He moved so she could see him more easily. "Only a few minutes, Samantha. Nothing to worry about."

"Felt like I was gone for hours."

He smiled. "Cool. Where did you go?"

"I'm not sure I remember it all. But I followed a magpie down below a thorny rose bush, down into the ground where I met Lulu. She held up a computer screen that said she was God Essence."

"Yeah," he said with a grin, "I know."

She sighed deeply. "What else do you know?"

"Everything I need to know," he said quickly. "There's so much information out there, Samantha. It's best just to know what you need. Don't go looking for trouble."

She was silent for a few minutes. She was aware of his presence beside her, slowly going through a tai chi routine. "Craig," she said finally.

He stopped exercising. "Uh huh?"

"What's wrong with me?"

"Nothing for you to worry about," he said firmly. "It's painful, I know, but the pain won't last long, and then I'll take you home. You'll recover quickly, and be back at work in no time."

"My car," she said, remembering. "We left my car on campus. Will we get back there this evening?"

"No, but I'll take care of it. I'll get my dad or somebody to drive over with me and we'll get your car back to your house tonight."

"Am I going to have to spend the night in the hospital?"

"I don't know, Samantha. Whatever happens, know there is purpose in it."

"Craig! My cat! You need to feed my cat."

Craig smirked. "Your cat could stand to lose some weight."

"Craig," she repeated in her authoritative teacher voice.

"Don't worry, Samantha. Of course I'll take care of your cat."

Another blurry figure came to take her to get the ultrasound then. "Do you want to come with us, sir?" the young man asked Craig.

"No," he said jovially. "Samantha, I'm going to head over to the cafeteria. See if they've got any pie."

Time and space moved quickly then, as unseen hands escorted her up and down dizzying halls. She could barely keep her eyes open as her belly was coated with KY jelly and fingers probed between her legs. Finally she was swathed in warm but thin blankets and a brown skinned man in a tie and white lab coat floated up to her side. She struggled to understand him. "Very rare," she heard him say.

"What?" she asked, trying to sit up.

"You needn't worry about the loss of one ovary," the doctor said. "The right ovary will take over the work of the other and you will continue to ovulate every month."

She felt panicky at this talk of ovaries. "What does that matter?" she blurted. "I'm sterile! It's a big waste of my time ovulating and menstruating at all!"

The doctor leaned closer. "Ms O'Malley, I don't know who told you you were sterile, but you wouldn't have a tubal pregnancy if you were sterile."

The man's face came into hyper focus. Samantha could see his prominent cheekbones, the enlarged pores around his nose, his wide brown eyes. "Tubal pregnancy? I have a tubal pregnancy?"

"That's why you are in so much pain. We must perform surgery immediately."

She felt her eyes welling up. "So I finally get pregnant, but I'm losing my baby? Just like that?"

The doctor took her hand. "I know it's upsetting to lose one of the twins. But the other will be fine. It will continue to grow and--"

"What?"

A disembodied voice from the other side of the room weighed in. "Doctor, it says here the patient didn't know she was pregnant."

"Oh!" The doctor was laughing now, and his face looked clownish and grotesque. Samantha wanted to swat at his jowly cheeks to make the noise stop. She balled up her hands to restrain herself. "What are you talking about?" she demanded.

"Samantha," the doctor said slowly, "You have a very rare condition. It's called a heterotopic pregnancy. You see, you are pregnant with twins, but one of the embryos has lodged in your left Fallopian tube. We will need to remove the left tube and ovary to save your life. Yes, your life depends on this surgery. But the other twin has implanted in your uterus and appears to be doing fine. There's no reason why this pregnancy won't come to term. You should give birth to a healthy baby in, oh, I'd say seven months."

The doctor's face was becoming very small and the lights in the room were twinkling. Samantha wasn't sure if she was crying or losing consciousness. "Ms O'Malley," she heard a voice address her from far away. "We need you to sign this consent form." A plastic pen was slipped between her fingers, but Samantha remembered nothing more.

***

The morning after her surgery, Samantha was awakened in her hospital room by a nurse hell-bent on getting her up and walking. She struggled to stand and stagger to the bathroom. They brought her a breakfast of scrambled eggs, toast with cream cheese, and canned peaches. Midmorning Craig came in, his jacket slung over his shoulder. "Morning, Ms O'Malley," he said. "You're looking rather spry. In fact you look so good, rumors are going to start circulating that you're quite the slacker."

"Oh, my God, Craig," she exclaimed. "I never called the school to tell them I wouldn't be in."

"Don't worry; I took care of it," he assured her. "I called that curmudgeonly secretary and told her you were in the hospital."

"What did they say when you told them, you know--"

"I didn't tell them anything. It's none of their business, Samantha."

She leaned her head back on the pillow. "They're going to think you're the father of my baby."

He shrugged. "You could do worse, Samantha. But by the way, if you're so worried what people think, maybe you should widen your circle when choosing boyfriend candidates."

Samantha gasped at his audacity. "I never told you—so what makes you think you know—I mean—oh, never mind!" She gnawed on the corner of her mouth. "I forgot who I was talking to."

He sat on the edge of her bed. "I'm not passing judgment, Samantha. You're passing judgment on yourself! When you let go of that, you won't give a second thought to what people think or don't think. It won't bother you at all."

"Good morning!" a cheery voice interrupted them. Samantha turned toward the door to see Anna Villaseñor standing there with a potted blue hydrangea in a wicker basket. "I hope I'm not interrupting anything."

"Not at all," Samantha said, assuming her professional demeanor, attempting to sit up and smooth her tangled hair.

"I'm Anna Villaseñor," the visitor said, extending her hand to Craig. "My daughter is in Samantha's class."

"Craig," the custodian said briefly as he accepted her handshake.

She smiled awkwardly at his brief introduction. "You must be Mr. O'Malley."

"Oh, no," Craig said quickly. "We're just friends. I work at the school too."

"What do you teach?" she asked pleasantly.

"I'm the night custodian," Craig said with obvious amusement. "I should be going."

"My father was a janitor," Anna interjected. "When he was quite young. Then he started his own custodial business. He employed a staff of fifteen men who cleaned office buildings in downtown Oakland. He was very proud of that company, and very proud that I chose to become a businesswoman as well."

Craig nodded. "Impressive," he acknowledged. Samantha noticed he was not so quick to leave now. In fact, he took the basket of flowers from Anna. "Let me put these on the shelf," he offered.

"They're beautiful," Samantha said. "That's so thoughtful of you."

"I won't stay long," Anna said. "I know you just had surgery last night, so I'm sure you're tired and in pain."

"How did you know about my surgery?" Samantha asked.

Anna smiled so broadly it seemed red lipstick would spread from her mouth to her teeth. "That's what I came to tell you: Luisa told me! She typed it to me. And then this morning I called the school, and confirmed you were here in Mercy General, well—I was so excited! I mean, of course I was concerned for you, but Samantha, there it is! There's our verification."

Samantha was dumbfounded. "You say she told you last night?"

"Yes," Anna said. "It wasn't right away. It was later in the evening when I was attempting to facilitate with her, and all of a sudden she started to type your name. She said, 'Ms O'Malley is having surgery tonight.' I couldn't believe it, but I thought where else could this be coming from if not from Luisa? I certainly don't have any knowledge of your health."

"What time was that?" Craig asked.

"Oh, about seven thirty, I guess," Anna replied.

Samantha sat up straighter. "But I don't know how she could have known that--"

Craig put his hand on her arm. "She must have overheard other staff members talking," he said.

"That would explain a lot," Anna agreed. "I thought, 'I can't believe they told the kids you had a tubal pregnancy.'" Samantha looked at Craig, her eyes frantic. Anna leapt in with a dismissive hand. "Oh, Samantha," she continued. "Don't worry; I won't tell anyone, and I certainly am not in a position to judge. I'm just glad you seem to be all right. And we finally have the verification we need."

Samantha nodded, her mouth slightly open in stunned surprise. "It's great news, Anna."

"I'm so thrilled, I feel like I'm walking on air!" Anna giggled like a schoolgirl. "Oh, I'm so sorry. I don't mean to be happy you're laid up here in the hospital. Which brings me to my next mission: are there any restrictions on your diet? We all know hospital food is not exactly haute cuisine. Now Anna Victoria's has come out with a wonderful line of potpies that are the perfect comfort food—especially when you need a pick me up! We've got chicken, turkey, beef, and this wonderfully savory Cuban pork pie. I can have one delivered within the hour—just in time for lunch. What would you like?"

"Beef sounds good," Craig said.

Samantha turned to him with her scolding teacher look. "Oh Anna, that's so generous, but I haven't much of an appetite yet. When I'm home in a day or two, I'll appreciate a few of those pies."

"That's okay, Samantha, I understand," she said. "But Craig, you'd like a beef pie? Shall I have that delivered here or to the school?"

"Oh, no—this is about Samantha. I can sample the pie when you send it to Samantha."

"They'll also be available in the freezer section of your local Raley's, Bel Air, and Nob Hill grocery stores within the next month," Anna added.

Anna left and Samantha lay silent, listening to the click of her high-heeled boots on the hospital linoleum as she strode down the hallway. She glanced at Craig, and he was waiting for the fading of her footfall as well. Finally she shook her head. "How?" she said simply with an exaggerated shrug. "How could Luisa have known? I mean yesterday evening at 7:30—well, I have no idea what I was doing at 7:30, but--"

"The doctor didn't even come out with a diagnosis till around eight o'clock," Craig told her. "You went into surgery around 9."

"Do you think people at school are speculating about why I'm here?" Samantha lamented to Craig.

"Samantha!" he laughed. "What if they are? It doesn't matter! And if they are, they couldn't have been saying anything that Lulu overheard because she left school yesterday at 2 o'clock. I didn't even drive you here to the hospital until nearly 3:30."

"This is so crazy!" Samantha said. "It makes me so tired."

"Don't be afraid of the information you've just been given!" Craig said insistently. "Yes, this is the verification you've been waiting for—but not that Lulu is able to facilitate. This is verification that Lulu is an advanced soul, come here to California on a mission of some kind. She most certainly is here to work with you, maybe with me too—it's impossible to know. But she's not just an intellect trapped in a body with tremendous physical limitations; she is also an advanced soul with clairvoyant abilities."

"But Craig, I'm here in the hospital. Now finally I'm given some sort of message, a message that reveals her identity, but I won't be back to work with her for three or four weeks or more. This seems like terrible timing."

"Everything is perfect, Samantha. Don't concern yourself with appearances. You are working with Lulu right now, I'm sure of it. You don't have to be in the same room with somebody to do spiritual work. Whatever energy the two of you are fashioning together—I don't know. But know that whatever the collective needs you to do—you have the skill to complete that work. That's why you're here. These things aren't random."

"But Craig--"

"Look Samantha, stop worrying! You have always worried so much! You are ready! Other people have tried to tell you this,

they've tried to reassure you, but you keep missing it! I'm here now.
It's all going to be okay. You will succeed."

CHAPTER EIGHTEEN

Samantha came home from the hospital the next day, happy to be back in her own bed with her cat for company. Though she had been living solo since the divorce, this was the first time she felt truly alone. Nowhere to go, no expectations to meet, no one to talk to: she knew the idleness would be restful and healing, or it would drive her to depression. She wasn't sure which face solitude would show her.

Like the disciplined teacher she was, she imposed a routine upon her days: rising at a reasonable hour to practice gentle yoga poses, a simple breakfast of raisin bran and milk, then a short walk in the neighborhood, going a little farther each day. In the afternoons she surrendered to the couch, watching old movies on cable and reading paperback novels. She refrained from gardening, vacuuming, and heavy thinking. She wondered about the baby, due in June as Craig had predicted. She knew she had a lot of plans that needed making, but she fell asleep whenever she contemplated the acquisition of a car seat, a crib, and a slew of baby clothes.

"I've been wanting a baby for years," she told Craig when he called. "So why aren't I happy? I ought to be ecstatic!"

"You're still recovering from surgery, Samantha. Give yourself time."

Co-workers brought casseroles, cookies and gossip. It seemed Bunny had disappeared the same day Samantha went into the hospital. Everyone wondered if Samantha knew anything about her special education cohort, but Samantha was as clueless as the rest of the staff. Everyone professed concern for Samantha's health, hinting that they wanted details. Samantha became practiced at rolling her eyes and lifting her shoulders in embarrassment. "Oh, you know," she'd say in a low voice, "female problems." She felt a little silly at her dramatized modesty, but she hadn't decided how to proceed. She knew she should call both Charlie and Jon, but the prospect made her very tired. Still she didn't want either of them to hear the news from someone else.

A week into her convalescence the phone rang. "Samantha," a familiar voice said, "it's Jon Convivio."

"Jon!" She said, unable to hide her surprise. "It's so good to hear from you."

"My daughter and I are in town to visit her cousins on her mother's side of the family. We're just here for two days, but I was wondering if you'd like to have lunch? I'm free both today and tomorrow, so whichever day you prefer. . ."

Samantha noticed the eager tone of his voice, and wondered if he wanted a little more than just lunch. "Oh, Jon, um—you know, I'm recovering from surgery and I don't feel much like going out today."

"Surgery," he said in a concerned voice. "I hope you're doing okay, Samantha. Was it serious?"

She paused for a moment to gather her courage, then forged ahead. "I guess it could have been, but it all turned out all right. Yeah, you see, I had a tubal pregnancy—and surprisingly enough, that fetus was a twin—so I'm still pregnant. Isn't that something?"

"That does sound serious," he said slowly.

"I was planning to contact you," she said, almost defensively. "I really felt you should know. . ."

She let her voice trail off, wondering what he'd say. "Oh, Samantha," he said, "I'm not sure how to put this, dear, but, uh, I'll try to be as delicate as possible. I need to ask, well—if you haven't had another partner recently? If not then I should visit my doctor to see why my vasectomy has somehow reversed itself!"

"Oh!" Samantha exclaimed in surprise, then she laughed. "Oh, my!"

She could hear him laughing too. "I hope you're not disappointed, dear."

"Oh, I hope this doesn't come out the wrong way," she admitted, "but I'm actually relieved."

Again he laughed. "No offense taken, Samantha; I understand."

"I've just been so embarrassed, because, you know--"

"Oh, Samantha," he said sympathetically, "you don't have to explain to me: you're just out of a marriage, and we all have needs. I certainly understand. Sylvia was so sick the two years before she died. I felt guilty as a new widower—but I had needs. I know what it's like."

Samantha felt herself tearing up, and she brushed a tear from her cheek. "Thank you, Jon."

"So listen, Samantha, we can still have lunch. I remember that deli near the school makes great food to go. I could bring you a care package—if you feel up to it."

"You're a true gentleman, Jon," she said. "Of course I feel up to seeing you. I look forward to it."

***

On Halloween Samantha was surprised to find Jenna Finch at her door, bearing a plate of Halloween candies and cookies. "The staff room is lousy with high caloric treats!" Jenna declared. "I hated for you to miss out."

Samantha grinned. She was eating for two now. Maybe an extra cookie or two wouldn't be so bad. "That's so thoughtful of you."

She invited Jenna in, offered her apple juice or tea. Jenna declined refreshments. "I won't stay long. But I'm aware there's been some gossip, and I wanted you to hear the straight story from me."

She paused and Samantha felt her heart leap into her throat, wondering if she had been the subject of these whispers. She raised her eyebrows, hoping to appear receptive rather than apprehensive.

"Well," Jenna continued, "Bunny Schwartz has taken a position in the district's adult education program. After the incident with your student, I spoke with the assistant superintendent and with the director of special education, and we all strongly urged her to take this offer. Fortunately she didn't require much persuasion. I'm grateful for that. It could have been messy, but it wasn't."

Samantha exhaled slowly. "That is good news," she acknowledged.

Jenna nodded. "In the next few weeks, I will be sending all of our special education personnel to Proactive Training—it's a three day seminar on how to prepare for and respond to aggressive behavior. The training includes how to appropriately intervene and restrain students when necessary. I'd like you to be trained as well when your doctor gives you permission to do so."

"I was trained years ago," Samantha said. "But I'm sure my certification is no longer valid."

"Well, I want everyone up to speed. I want everyone on staff to be aware of what's legal, what's effective and what's appropriate."

"That's great, Jenna," Samantha told her. "I'm grateful you're addressing this issue head on."

Jenna leaned forward. "And after you're trained, Samantha, I want you to make a presentation at a staff meeting. Something brief—twenty to thirty minutes or so. Obviously it's not necessary to teach everyone how to restrain kids. But everyone needs to know how *not* to restrain kids. I don't need any more loose cannons out there hot dogging it. I want it very clear that's not okay."

"Oh, I agree, Jenna," Samantha said slowly, reluctant to share any secrets yet. "But it could be a while before I'm able to be trained. Couldn't someone else brief the staff?"

Jenna pursed her lips. "I'd really like it to be you, Samantha. But we'll see what evolves." The young principal seemed to deliberately turn the conversation to Samantha and her health, how she was feeling, how soon she expected to be back. Samantha kept the banter light, focusing on exercise, diet, and the dearth of intelligence on daytime TV. Jenna recommended a few movies, Samantha bragged that she'd managed to re-read a few classics during her time recuperating on the couch. Then the doorbell rang. The first trick-or-treaters had arrived. Jenna took her leave.

***

It was the Saturday before Samantha was scheduled to return to work. Midafternoon, around three o'clock, she sat on the couch, a paperback novel open in her hands, but her mind racing above and beyond any prose on the page. As if summoned by this restless rumination, Charlie Easter called.

He was all bluster and bravado, his voice booming like the emcee at some big league sporting event, chanting her many titles as soon as she answered the phone: "Ms O'Malley! How good to hear the voice of the elusive and enchanting Ms Omm, the mysterious Samjan, celebrated teacher of the century, Samantha O'Malley! How you doing, Sam?"

And just like that any resolve she may have had to be noncommittal, aloof or even business-like all went out the door. He took her breath away as he always had, and like a nervous teenager she found herself stammering, almost gasping for breath. "Charlie! Hi, how are you?"

"I'm hanging in here, Sam. I am learning what it means to persevere! And how are you Sam? You doing okay?"

She paused for a moment, floored by his verbosity and stunned by this simple question: how are you? *How am I?* she wondered, but she couldn't tell him, not yet. Maybe in a minute or two, her courage would catch up with her and she'd be able to break the news. But right now she heard herself feigning an enthusiasm she did not feel. "I'm good, Charlie. I'm doing just fine. Just sitting here reading a book. Really good."

"Good book, huh?"

"Yeah," she reiterated, feeling a little silly. "Really good."

"Hey, Sam," he said. "I don't see you on Twitter anymore."

"Twitter?" she repeated stupidly, wondering why Twitter would be his priority. His mother was ill, possibly dying, they hadn't spoken in weeks, but the first thing he does is ask about Twitter?

"Letting the Twitter account slide?" he asked.

"Um, yeah," she blundered on, still hoping to get her feet under this conversation. "You know what, Charlie? I've—uh—I've been ill lately, and I just haven't checked in on Twitter. I'm sorry. I hope I haven't missed anything important."

"No, nothing important, Sam. Just, you know, a little chatter."

She licked her lips, determined to launch the conversation in a new direction. "Okay, Charlie, but tell me about you. How are you? How's your Mom?"

"Oh, Sam," he lamented, "a lot of ups and downs. Some days she's got all this energy. She amazes the nurses and the physical therapist. Other days she's sullen and dark. She refuses to get out of bed, argues with everybody. She's just an old crab. So you know, it's rough going over to the nursing home because I never know which Adelaine Easter is going to show up!"

Samantha drew a deep breath. "I'm sorry, baby," she said. "That sounds so hard."

"Some days," he said. "Some days it is."

"How are things between the two of you, Charlie? After all, you've lived on separate coasts for a couple of decades or more. Are you getting along okay?"

"Yeah, sure, it's okay, Sam. It's so different from how it used to be."

"What do you mean?"

"Well," he said, drawing out the word. "She's so small."

"She always was pretty short," she reminded him.

"Yeah, I know, Sam, that's not what I'm talking about." He paused. "You see, my mother had this tremendous spirit. Sure, she was barely five feet tall but when she came through the door everybody sat up and looked her way. Now, I don't know, she's just so small. She's thin and frail. Some days she's cheerful, some days she's angry—doesn't matter, she's not herself. She's small. Maybe the mighty part of her has already left."

She could hear his voice cracking and she felt a deep yearning for him in her gut. "Wow, Charlie," she said. "I'm so sorry."

"Thanks, Sam," he said brusquely, his voice hoarse but strong again. "But hey, how are you? You say you've been sick?"

His boisterous question pulled her back. She couldn't do it. She couldn't tell him, not with everything else he was going through. That's what she told herself anyway. "I'm fine," she lied. "I'm getting better."

"Some virus going around?" he asked.

"That's right," she said, glad for this convenient excuse. "Something like that. It hit me pretty hard, but I'm much better now."

"So maybe I'll get you back on Twitter, girl. You know you can set it to connect with your cell phone so the phone will alert you when you get a tweet."

Twitter again. What was up with that? Short, impersonal messages: was that his preferred mode of communicating with her? She felt a heaviness descend on her chest. He was three thousand miles away and he was not interested in a deep connection with her. But she wasn't interested in a casual one with him.

"You know, Charlie, I never got much into Twitter to begin with. After all, I am definitely not SamJan."

"That's true. You need a new Twitter handle. How about @MsOmm? That would be perfect for you."

"Oh, I don't know," she said, feeling a little annoyed with all the Twitter talk. "Maybe I'll just close the Twitter account. You can call or email if you want to contact me."

"Oh, Sam," he blurted suddenly. "I really miss you, girl!"

She nearly dropped the phone. First he's urging her onto a social media site that would limit their exchanges to 140 public characters, and now he announces an affectionate longing for her? "What?" she said, unable to accept his proclamation at face value.

"I just may fall for you again!" he exclaimed.

Her heart seemed to bound into her throat. "I—I don't even know what you mean by that," she said hopefully.

"I don't know either, Sam," he said. "I wish I could be there with you, but I need to be here now. Here with my Mom. Being with you again—gosh, how long ago was it? Labor Day weekend? It was, wasn't it?"

"Yeah," she confirmed. "That's when we—you know--"

"That's when we made love. Yeah, Sam, you know being with you again reminded me of loyalty."

"Loyalty," she repeated blankly, disappointed that she had evoked such an unromantic virtue, more reminiscent of a boy scout perhaps. "Loyalty?"

"You used to say that I needed to learn loyalty," he began.

"Oh, Charlie," she interrupted, "let's not dredge up the past. Not now."

"But you were right," he insisted. "I do need to work on loyalty. You're loyal. You're loyal to your students. You bend over backwards to help them. Shoot, you're not even married anymore, but I couldn't get you to say anything disparaging about your ex-husband. Not even a little gossip about his campaigns or his catered parties. See, that's loyalty. So here I am thinking I need to be loyal to Mom. She wasn't always the perfect mother but she did the best she could. She deserves my loyalty. In a way, I feel like I'm doing it for you, Sam. To show you I was paying attention. That I was a good student."

Samantha felt exhausted, as if she'd been riding a roller coaster in the dark, unaware when the car might make a vertical ascent or plummet to the depths. Did he miss her, love her, want her?—or were his feelings best summed up as some kind of noble admiration? "Well," she managed, "I guess I can't escape my true calling. I'm first and foremost a teacher."

"You're more than that to me, Sam," he said quickly. "You know that, don't you?"

No, she wanted to shout, *I don't know who or what I am to you! You've made your feelings as muddy as always, and I have no way to discern the truth.* If she told him about the baby, maybe the ambivalence would clear up: he would step up or back off. But she wanted him to want her for herself. Accepting or rejecting fatherhood would be step two. She couldn't risk a showdown right now. Not when he was three thousand miles away.

"I'm proud of you, Charlie," she said, finally resigned to stay cast in the teacher role he had assigned her. "I'm glad you're back there in New England where you need to be now, supporting your mom. I know it's hard, but you'll never regret giving her this time. You never will."

"Thanks, Sam," he said softly. "I know you're right."

CHAPTER NINETEEN

Samantha dressed in bright autumn colors, teal and orange, for her first day back at work. Determined to keep a positive attitude she reminded herself that new principal Jenna had proved to be an assertive ally, Bunny would no longer haunt her door, and she would get to chat with Craig most days when he came in to vacuum her classroom. Concerns about single motherhood would take care of themselves with a few prayers. Right now she wanted to enjoy the children in her class.

But leave it to Echo Abernathy to give her a strong shot of reality. "You can't make me," Echo taunted when Samantha presented her with a new worksheet less than an hour after the day began. Samantha's heart sank. *Oh, yeah, I remember what this is like.* She threw back her shoulders, pushed the hair away from her face and launched into a sincere attempt at faux indifference. "No problem, Echo," she said coolly. "You can do it at recess."

Echo slumped in her chair, threw a sweater over her head and spent the better part of the morning in deep pout.

At recess, alone in the room with Echo, Samantha presented the girl with a series of independent tasks to complete to compensate for her defiant idleness. "Here are your choices," Samantha informed the child. "Do your work now and you might still earn enough points to earn computer games here this afternoon and the Wii at home tonight. Or do nothing and lose points."

"I don't care," Echo snapped.

Samantha sank into the chair at her desk, holding her breath, unwilling to reveal any disappointment or frustration. She managed a half smile as she clicked on her own computer. "Whatever, Echo," she said with forced bravado. "It's your choice."

Samantha heard Echo snort, but the girl was quiet so she could safely ignore her. Or rather she could pretend to ignore her. As she often told her aides, never ever ignore a child, but pretending to ignore—now that's a great form of behavior management.

She dug in her tote bag for a Granny Smith apple and took a hefty bite. Turning her attention to the computer again she logged on to a website of baby names she had taken to visiting. This would be a bigger responsibility than naming a cat, but it would also be more fun.

"They fired Mrs. Schwartz," Echo announced. "Did you know that?"

Samantha glanced up briefly, not wanting to give Echo any attention, but wanting to set the record straight. "They did not fire Mrs. Schwartz, Echo. She chose to take another job."

"Uh uh," Echo said in a smug taunt. "They did so fire her. They fired her for what she did to me!"

Shocked at this assertion, Samantha looked over at Echo. Echo's mouth and chin looked like a fist: raised, clenched and defiant. Samantha held her breath, wondering where Echo had heard this gossip, but also aware that her intel was pretty close to the mark. Still she did not want Echo to think she had that kind of power, that she could throw a full-on, thrashing, cussing, knock-your-socks-off tantrum and get a teacher fired. She cleared her throat. "Echo," she said slowly, "Mrs. Schwartz—with Mrs. Finch's help—decided that she would do better working with grown-ups instead of with kids. So now she's teaching adults. She didn't get fired." She paused, unsure if she should say anything more. "And that's all you or anyone else needs to know," she added. At that she clicked off the computer, sensing her attention was needed elsewhere. She munched on her apple, sneaking glances at Echo, watching the girl stare at her own hands.

After a long pause, Echo spoke in a squeaky voice. "I thought-" Her voice cracked. "I thought they fired you too."

She began to whimper, tears sliding down her cheeks in what seemed a sincere display of genuine emotion. Samantha stood up and came to Echo's desk. "Oh, no sweetie; they didn't fire me. I got sick very suddenly. I was in the hospital. Mrs. Finch came in and talked to you kids, didn't she? Rose told me she did. Weren't you here that day?"

"I was here--but so what!" Echo blurted, angry now. "They told me my Mom was sick too. But she wasn't sick. She was in jail."

Samantha felt her own eyes tear up at the magnitude of this child's baggage. She sat down to pat her back and squeeze her shoulders. "Echo, I'm so sorry. You've had a lot of awful things happen to you. But you need to focus on *now*. Your mom is back and she's working hard so she can stay with you! And I'm back too."

Echo sniffled and cleared her throat. "Yeah, but you're going to leave again."

Samantha leaned back, afraid the girl was slipping into theatrical manipulation mode. "Echo," she scolded gently, "I'm not planning to leave--"

"Oh, yes, you are!" Echo interrupted. "When you have your baby you'll leave."

Samantha sat bolt upright, adrenaline blasting in her throat and solar plexus. "Who told you that?" she asked.

"Nobody had to tell me," Echo countered. "I can see—your tits are getting all big just like my mom's did when she was first pregnant with Phoebe."

Samantha sat stiffly for a moment, her cheeks hot and her head light. She was most definitely not ready to make an announcement to her students and coworkers. She looked over at Echo, expecting smugness, but Echo looked scared. "Are you all right, Ms O'Malley?"

Samantha laid her cheek in her hand. "Please get me some water, Echo."

Echo scurried off and returned with a paper cup filled with liquid. Samantha was surprised but grateful that Echo knew where to find the cup. She sipped slowly, wondering what to say, wondering if she should say anything. As she so often did with her students, she just started talking. "Echo, you've had a very hard life. I know you've got a lot you're still dealing with, stuff you will always have to deal with. But I'm putting you on notice right now: that doesn't mean you get to talk to me or anyone else this way. It is very impolite to make comments like you just did about someone's body. You understand?"

Echo nodded. "Sorry."

Samantha took another sip of water. "My plan is to be here until the end of the school year—at least! I signed a contract saying I would do that. And your Mom signed a contract for you—it's called an Individual Education Plan, an IEP—and it says you'll be here in my class until the end of this school year too. So we will be together, for better or worse, unless some strange event interferes."

"Like what?" Echo asked.

"I don't know," Samantha said with a smile, finally feeling a little playful. "Maybe there'll be a flood and we'll have to have class on a boat."

"That might be fun," Echo said hopefully.

Samantha rolled her eyes as she stood up. "Get to work, Echo," she directed.

"Okay," Echo agreed, and she picked up her pencil.

***

"I missed you," Lulu typed to Samantha that afternoon.

"I missed all you kids too," Samantha said in a non-committal way, then she switched to typing herself. "Have you done any reading since I've been out?"

Lulu rocked in her chair then reached for Samantha's hand. "I read a book about lamas," she typed.

"Llamas?" Samantha said aloud. Then she started to type. "Do you mean llamas like the animal in South America, or lamas like in Tibetan Buddhism—you know, like the Dali Lama?"

"Lamas," Lulu typed again.

Samantha stared at the page. This was not helpful. She did not want to guide her hand. She listened to an animated Pocahontas singing to John Smith on the TV in the front of the room. She'd only been back one day from sick leave and she was already resorting to Disney movies. This was too easy a habit to fall into. She was going to have to figure out a way to do this with Lulu without neglecting the other children. The bigger question was whether or not this was a worthwhile activity to do with Lulu—academically speaking. If Lulu were indeed here for some sort of energetic purpose, well, that couldn't be Samantha's concern, could it? Or should that be her main concern? Clarity was not something she was currently blessed with.

"Tell me about the lamas," Samantha said diplomatically.

Lulu grasped her hand in a tight clutch. "The lamas are pack animals. They traverse the narrow mountain passes through the Peruvian Andes with their sure footed gait."

Samantha looked with amazement at the textbook lilt in Lulu's typing. This did not sound like something she herself would write, so certainly she couldn't be guiding her hand, could she? She took a deep breath. Why was she still so scared about that?

"You were born in Peru, weren't you, Lulu?" Samantha typed.

The speed and velocity of Lulu's rocking increased. "Yes," she typed. "I was born in a city at the base of the Andes. My birth mother died in childbirth. She was very young, and had been disowned by her parents when she became pregnant out of wedlock. I was taken to an orphanage."

"That's very sad about your birth mother," Samantha typed. She was afraid to voice her thoughts out loud, for fear of showing too much emotion and scaring Lulu away from her story. "Does it make you feel sad to think about her?"

"No," Lulu typed. "She was a very advanced soul, and she is

greatly honored for the service she performed for me. She had a very short, very hard life—in some ways very ugly. Her older brother wanted to sell her into prostitution when she was 11. He would have gotten a high price from a European tourist who would have paid him in euros for the thrill of deflowering a virgin. But then her brother discovered she was already pregnant by one of her schoolmates, a local Indian boy, only 13 years old. Her brother wanted to kill the boy who was my father, but he escaped into the mountains. Perhaps I will see him again. I sense he and I still may have work to do together. He took my mother at an early age because he wanted to protect her, but he was too young."

"This is a disturbing story," Samantha typed. "I sense you were not told this story on the physical planes, but that you only know it because you--" She stopped typing, unsure what to say. She thought for a moment then set her fingers on the keys once more. "You intuit this information somehow—is that correct?"

"Yes, the information comes to me because it is time for me to know it," Lulu typed. "No one in a physical vehicle has ever shared this information—at least not using the conventional means of communication. I suspect the information may have come through my adoptive mother, Anna, but I cannot be certain of this at this time. I believe she is aware of this story." The girl paused, dropping her hands into her lap as she began to rock again. Suddenly she grabbed Samantha's hand. "You could tell her this story," Lulu suggested, "and see what she says. This would be a good means of verification for you. Since you are so concerned with verification."

Samantha drew back for a moment. "I don't think that's a good idea," she said in a low voice. "If Anna knows this story, she will be shocked that you know it. If she doesn't know the story, she'll think I've made up something fanciful, and it may only convince her that I'm guiding your hand."

Lulu grabbed her hand and immediately resumed typing. "Is that what you thought when you discovered I'd told her about your tubal pregnancy?"

"No, that's not what I thought," she said aloud. Then she began to type. "I saw it as verification that you are an advanced soul, here for a purpose."

"Each of us is here for a purpose, Ms Omm." Samantha swallowed hard, seeing Lulu had used Charlie's nickname for her. Perhaps it was a typo, or coincidence.

"I am not an advanced soul," Lulu continued. "This is my first life time, the first time this energetic signature has taken a physical form. I am pure God essence. I am unfiltered divinity, unshaped by the past life times that bring karma and burdens and presuppositions to the rest of you. You, Ms Omm, have been incarnating in this physical form for hundreds of thousands of years. I guess you must enjoy it."

"I don't know about that," Samantha muttered. Lulu released a sudden burst of laughter and squeezed Samantha's hand tight.

"You are an energetic master and you have reached a high degree of specialization," she typed. "You are needed here."

Samantha stared at the page a long time, wondering what she should say or do, what questions she should ask. She was intrigued, but she was also tired. "Is there something you think I should be doing?" she whispered finally.

"It is never about doing," Lulu typed. "It is about being."

"But why are you here?" Samantha typed. "In my dream you said you had come to learn from me—but I have nothing to teach."

"I am learning from you now," Lulu typed. "Our energetic exchange which occurs when we are in close proximity is very helpful to me. My cellular capacity is expanding exponentially."

Again Samantha leaned back and stared at the page. This was way over her head. Then the bell rang and she sprang to her feet. "Oh no, I lost track of the time! We're going to be late for the bus! We better get a move on."

Rose and Valerie quickly handed out homework folders and backpacks. Craig came in through the media center door and gave her a silent greeting with a nod of his head. Escaping from Samantha's hold, Lulu rushed over to him, and placed an upturned right palm at his heart chakra. He lifted a hand as if coaxing her to give him a high five, and she complied, using her left hand. Then she lifted her right hand and he swatted it with his left. She lifted her knee, bumping against his outer thigh. He lifted his knee, gently brushing against her outer thigh. She directed her left elbow again his midsection, and he returned the favor. She tapped his left shoulder with her right hand, and he tapped her right shoulder with his left hand. Their strange dance continued like this for a few moments more, she squealing with peals of giggling laughter, he chuckling in delighted surprise. Finally she reached her right hand forward and planted her palm on his chest. He allowed her this hold for a few seconds, then took her hand and squeezed it. "You've got to catch the bus," he said gently. She flew away from him, darting across the room where Samantha waited by the back door. She gazed into Samantha's eyes for a moment, then reached up to touch Samantha's cheek. Samantha looked at Lulu expectantly, realizing she would not be surprised if the girl began speaking in iambic pentameter. But Luisa glanced away and the moment passed. Samantha looked over at Craig. "We better go to the bus," she said, disappointed. "I'll talk to you later." He nodded.

CHAPTER TWENTY

Craig was vacuuming in the empty classroom when Samantha returned from the bus stop. She flipped off the light switch to get his attention, then watched in amusement as he glanced first overhead, then back her way.

He turned off the vacuum cleaner and laughed. "Cute trick," he said appreciatively but Samantha ignored the compliment.

"What just happened?" she demanded.

Craig shrugged. "Well, you fooled me into thinking the power had gone out, and yet the vacuum cleaner was still working—"

"No, no—what happened with Lulu? She had such a look of expectation on her face! I was sure she was going to speak."

"She may do that soon," Craig said in a serious voice. "That could happen. But Samantha, the point is it doesn't matter!" He left the vacuum in the center of the room and walked toward her. "She may go through her so-called life on this earth plane in complete silence. She may start typing independently, or begin speaking. She might become a media phenomenon, appearing on the Today Show and the Oprah network. Maybe she'll do a Pepsi commercial or star in a movie. Or she may become known as the spiritual avatar that she is truly is. She could attract huge crowds in stadiums and arenas." He gestured dramatically with his long fingers. "Any of those things could happen. But—she might live her life in her present guise, as a child--and then as a woman--with grave physical limitations, as an individual with autism, and no one will ever know how intelligent and clever and funny she is."

"But Craig, surely that won't happen."

He smiled as he reached over and turned the lights back on. "Samantha, don't you see? It doesn't matter! She will accomplish the work she came to do whether anyone knows about it or not. In fact, perhaps it will be easier for her that way. No distractions. It's certainly not your call—and the Craig vehicle hasn't got a clue what's going to happen."

Samantha winced. "Really?" she said doubtfully. "Not a clue?"

He rolled his eyes and lifted his hands in surrender. "Okay: I see many potentials. But it's most likely that she will do her work in obscurity. That really is the most likely outcome."

Samantha sank into a chair at Rose's workstation. "I'm sure you're right that that would be easiest," she conceded.

He grinned. "But you're disappointed."

"No," she said firmly.

He raised his eyebrows, and she shrugged in defeat. "I'm not disappointed, that's for sure. It's just--" She looked up at him slowly. "I don't know—I'd like a sign—just a little sign--"

"You'd like verification," he said. "That's what you've been saying all along."

"Yes!" she exclaimed.

"I can understand that," he conceded. "Because you don't know if I'm just some crazy guy, or if I really am the genuine article. You'd like something tangible. Something you can hold in your hands."

"Is that too much to ask?" she said theatrically, laughing at her own melodramatic demeanor.

He nodded thoughtfully. "Let me tell you a story," he said. "A parable, if you will."

She settled back in her chair.

"Imagine," he said, "a soul between life times, neither male nor female, resting on the astral planes, as I said, between life times. And the soul says to—whomever—the powers-that-be--"

"St. Peter, maybe?" Samantha interjected.

Craig gestured broadly toward her. "Perfect. So the soul says to St. Peter: 'I want to cure polio!' And St. Peter says, 'That's very admirable, but also very ambitious. It will take a lot of hard work.' The soul says, 'No matter. I'll do whatever it takes.' So this soul goes forth!" He swung both hands up like a conductor.

"And becomes Jonas Salk," Samantha said.

"Don't jump ahead," Craig scolded. Samantha shrugged with mock innocence. "Jonas Salk did not become Jonas Salk in one life time," he informed her.

"Sorry," she said, humble this time. He continued.

"So this soul worked for many incarnations as a humble human deeply affected by polio. He—or she—suffered from polio, died of polio, watched her children die of polio. Finally St. Peter said, 'This is it! This will be the incarnation during which you will have a major break-through.'"

"Finally Jonas Salk?" she asked.

"This soul I'm telling you about," Craig countered, "was born a female. She grew up in a poor family and married a man who was not worthy of her. They had two or three children and then her husband deserted her. But she was hard working and generous of spirit. She worked as a waitress in a small coffee shop and she put her kids through college." He paused to raise an index finger as if sensing Samantha's confusion. "Here's the thing: every day, Jonas Salk came into that coffee shop and had lunch or a cup of coffee and pie—whatever. The waitress and the scientist were in close proximity. Maybe they exchanged pleasantries, maybe more than that—doesn't matter. But every minute of every day that waitress was channeling spiritual energy to Jonas Salk and his colleagues. She was the focal point for that energy. Years later after they had all dropped their bodies, the soul who had played the role of Jonas Salk came to the soul who had played the role of the waitress and said, 'It was a privilege working under you. You directed the energy flawlessly.'" Craig concluded with a quick nod as he spread his hands.

"Wow," Samantha said. "That's a wonderful story. Is it true?"

"Yes," Craig said firmly. "Of course it's true." He picked up a wastebasket near Rose's station. "Whether or not this story manifested in exactly that way I can't be sure. But of course it's true. I wouldn't tell you something that wasn't true."

He turned to dump the wastebasket in the can on his cart, and she rose to follow him. "I get it," she said. "We all have our jobs to do and our roles to play." He turned to face her and she gave him a sly smile. "But if I was that waitress—I don't know—I'd like a sign, a teeny, tiny sign!"

"Oh, Samantha," he said laughing. "What about a miracle pregnancy—that's not enough for you?"

"Gee, Craig," she blurted immediately. "I don't know."

"Be honest, Samantha," he said in a challenging voice. "It's not the baby that's a miracle. It's the feeling you're beginning to have about the baby coming—that's the miracle."

"What do you mean?"

He nodded slowly, looking off into the distance. "You're beginning to feel more confident than you've ever felt in your entire life, aren't you? C'mon admit it! You're beginning to feel happier than you've felt in your entire life too. I know, it's a scary prospect, having a baby alone. But you're feeling optimistic, you're feeling happy."

She looked down, trying to stifle a smile. "It's probably just the second trimester hormones." Then she looked up at him, a little frantic. "What if the hormones are giving me a false sense of security—a false sense of ability? Can I really do this?"

"Samantha," he said, reaching out to squeeze her hand. "Trust your heart. You know you are entering an adventure you've been longing for your entire adult life. This is what you've been waiting around for. This is why you're still here."

"Why? Because of my baby or because of my work with Lulu?"

He shrugged as he headed off to get another wastebasket to empty. "Well, I can't be sure, but I don't think there's any separation," he said. "Avatars usually incarnate in threes, you know."

"What are you saying?"

"Well," he continued as he emptied more garbage. "I'm not saying anything really. It's just I couldn't help thinking about that when the doctor said you had been carrying twins."

"What!" she exclaimed. "Are you saying that I was carrying the other two entities that were to make up a trinity? But then I lost one of them!"

"Samantha," Craig said gently. "You didn't lose that baby: that entity made the choice to experience what amounted to a spontaneous abortion, and now it will incarnate in a different way. Know that these are things the Samantha vehicle does not control, but also know that as your higher self, the God essence that is the true Samantha, you have participated in creating and executing this plan. You have not only consented to these life events—you helped plan them. Know that it's perfect. It can't go wrong."

"Yeah, I guess," she said softly as she sank into the nearest chair, this time at Valerie's station. Craig chuckled at her seeming reluctance to accept what he was saying. Shaking his head, he returned to the vacuum cleaner.

Samantha sat silently watching Craig push the machine methodically across the carpet. His face was smooth and serene-looking, as if this daily chore was not a tedious task but a walking meditation. Following his lanky form with her eyes she drifted into a hypnotic stare, and the room seemed to glow with blue light. Without effort or intent she imagined an anthem of yellow-billed magpies, a dozen or more, collected to reassure her that she was in the right place. But was it really as simple as Craig claimed? Would life proceed in perfect order no matter what she did? No, wait, that's not quite what he'd been telling her. She still had to do the work. But the work was right in front of her. She didn't have to search for it. She didn't have to reinvent herself as bear, jaguar, or giraffe. She was ready, here and now, and she would know what to do when the time was right. She just needed to trust in the power of her own Inner Divinity to guide her.

He turned off the vacuum cleaner and her vision of magpies dissolved. She stood up. "Thank you," she said.

"For what?"

"For being here," she told him. "I'm so happy you're here."

He shrugged humbly as he wound up the vacuum cord. "You're welcome."

"I'm really tired," she said as she strode across the room to retrieve her purse. "I'm going to go home."

"You should," Craig agreed. "You need more rest now."

She pulled on her jacket and turned to him. "Craig, be honest."

"Always," he promised.

She turned her profile toward him. "Am I starting to show yet?"

He squinted. "I know you're pregnant, so it's apparent to me. But I don't think it's obvious. A few of the older women on the staff have noticed, but they haven't said anything to anyone."

"But they've talked to you!"

"Oh, no," he said hastily. "No one has."

"Well, then, how do you know they're—oh, never mind."

He grinned. "I don't want to hear people's thoughts but sometimes when I'm walking down the hall, they're thinking really loud!" He laughed. "Samantha, don't worry about it. These people like you, and they're concerned about you. Some of these women are concerned that your weight gain has something to do with your mysterious surgery. They'll be so relieved to find out you don't have some rapidly growing tumor inside your belly! Trust me, they all want to be aunties to this baby you're going to have. I can see it."

"Really?"

"Believe it! You are in a good place."

"Okay," she said happily as she slung her purse over her shoulder.

"All rightee then," he agreed.

"Craig?" she said again.

"Ye-es?" he said, comically drawing out the word.

"What was that little game you were playing with Lulu there right after the bell rang? That was very weird."

He nodded and sighed as if unsure whether to tell her. "She was programming me," he said solemnly.

"Programming you?"

"She was embedding instructions inside each of my cells—instructions I will need for ascension," he said simply, as if it were the most obvious thing in the world.

"What does that mean?"

"It was as if she were providing the rhythm to my harmony," he said, gesturing with his long fingers. "Her vehicle seems to be setting the pace for what is to come."

"Well," Samantha said slowly and deliberately, "what is to come?"

"The ascension of the earth realm to a place of great harmonic attraction—essentially the entire planet will shift through magnetic resonance into an alternate universe which will be more conducive to greater spiritual expansion."

Samantha sat down and rested her head in her hands. "Or," she said with a twinge of sarcasm, "the end of the world as we know it?"

"Maybe," he said laughing, "or maybe no one will notice."

"Well, gee, Craig," she said shaking her head and laughing, "if no one is going to notice, then what's the point? I mean is this one of those 2012 things that the Mayans supposedly concocted for us poor unsuspecting future humans after we've fucked everything on earth to hell and gone?"

He smiled and gave her a scolding look, "Ms O'Malley sounds awfully tired!"

"I am tired," she proclaimed. "I'm tired of all this talk about spiritual advancement and things getting better. Sure, I'm happy I'm going to have this baby; I'm afraid to say that aloud, lest the universe wreak more havoc for me. Because really—I'd just like to have a peaceful life. I don't want to do or be something special. I just want a humble little life. Is that too much to ask?"

He laughed. "A minute ago you were begging me for a sign! *Just a simple sign, Craig! Is that too much to ask?*"

"Oh, shut up," she said, teasing. "You're right; I'm tired. I'm going to go home."

"Let me carry your tote bag to the car for you," he offered.

"Okay."

"You know, Samantha," he said as they walked out the back door, "people may not notice ascension, but they will definitely begin to see a difference in the earth realm. Colors will seem brighter, the sky will appear a deeper shade of blue, and the sun will seem a deeper yellow with a twinge of orange to it."

"It will look like a giant peach," she said gleefully.

He chuckled despite her sarcastic tone. "As a matter of fact, it will," he said brightly. "And the people you love—the people you're meant to be with--they will appear to have a halo around their bodies."

"Just a big yellow halo, huh?"

"Maybe yellow, that's certainly traditional, but it might be any color of the spectrum—it could be pink or green or blue, even a rainbow. You'll notice it."

She unlocked the car doors as they approached her car. "Could you put that behind my seat?" she asked as she opened the driver's door.

He quickly obliged then turned to face her. "Of course," he said, "if it was up to me, everyone would have blue halos, since that's my favorite color."

"I like turquoise," she said.

"That's a little fancy for my taste," he responded.

"Amethyst is fancy," she informed him. "Turquoise would be just right."

"If you say so."

CHAPTER TWENTY-ONE

Anna had her secretary call and make an appointment to come in to see Samantha. Samantha was surprised and a little worried. This was not Anna's modus operandi. She preferred to make a grand entrance preceded and followed by the presentation of a boxed pie. This must be serious.

Samantha made time to clean up the classroom before Anna's arrival. She hung up a Christmas wreath or two, and wiped down the tables. It wasn't much, but it was all she had the energy for.

Anna arrived in a green velvet dress with a cowl neck and a red wool cape. She looked like Mrs. Claus—if Mrs. Claus were the CEO of a baking empire. Her fingernails were a brilliant candy apple red, and her hair was swept back in a long braid.

They sat at the table at the front of the room, a box of Kleenex between them since Samantha felt like she was getting a cold. She'd been sneezing all day.

"Our new pie shop did very well over Thanksgiving, and even though it's still a few weeks till Christmas, our figures show a healthy market share, much more than we'd expect for a new shop in town. We've also made inroads into local restaurants; we'll be supplying two local chains starting in January, as well as three catering businesses." She spoke as if reporting before the board of directors.

Samantha nodded with a silent half smile, wondering what this had to do with her. "Congratulations," she said quietly.

"Things were going so well," Anna continued, "that I had made a surprising decision." She paused theatrically. "I've been planning to leave the west coast operation in the hands of my very capable assistant. I want to move back east with Luisa, so she may work with one of the leaders in the field of facilitated communication. I've been planning to leave in January."

"Wow, that soon?" Samantha said in a stilted voice. "Well, that would certainly be a good move for Luisa. That's shows a lot of dedication that you would put your business on the back burner--"

"Well, it's not exactly the back burner," Anna said quickly. "I'll be scouting out locations for a new line of east coast operations. Sizing up the competition back there. It's a part of the business I haven't done in a long while. It will be a refreshing change of pace for me."

"So that works out well for both of you," Samantha said pleasantly, secretly feeling a bit relieved that she herself would be off Anna's radar. It had been hard living up to Anna's demands.

"Now, Samantha," Anna said, leaning forward across the table. "My plan includes you."

"Excuse me?" Samantha blurted, sitting up a little straighter. "I don't understand."

"No, I'm sure you understand a great deal more than anyone else—that's why I want you to be part of my operation," Anna said smoothly. "What I'm proposing will be a big change for you, but please hear me out." She paused for effect, eyebrows raised, hands lifted above the table as if ready to conduct a symphony.

Samantha said nothing, but Anna still waited. "Okay," she said obediently.

"I want you to come with us as Luisa's personal tutor. I will pay you whatever this school district pays you, plus 50 per cent."

"That's very generous," Samantha said, "but really, I'm not looking to move."

"Of course not, I understand. I would pay your moving expenses." She nodded, pointing what was supposed to be a reassuring finger at Samantha. "I treat my people right. In fact you have my permission to talk to anyone in my operation; I give you full access. I'm sure they'll all tell you I'm a good boss."

"Well, I don't doubt that--"

"No, but you're wondering: what will I have to do to earn 50 per cent more than I'm making here?" She lifted her chin. "I know teaching is a demanding job, especially a class like this one. You're probably wondering if I'll make your job 50 per cent harder. Well, you don't have to worry about that. I would expect a forty-hour workweek, which we could arrange in whatever way suits you. You might be working with Luisa at home, or when we're on the road. You might be with her in a public school classroom, acting as her personal aide, or perhaps you'll be studying with Professor Bidwell at the college. But no more than 40 hours a week. I really believe in that for my people. I want you to have a life."

"Again, Anna, this is all very kind of you, but--"

"I also know you're concerned about your baby," Anna interrupted.

Samantha's mouth dropped open.

"I'm sorry," Anna said, "was that supposed to be a secret? You all do a very poor job of keeping secrets from the kids here."

"I guess we do," Samantha said, shrugging awkwardly. "I'll need to talk to my aides about this."

"At any rate, Samantha," Anna went on, not missing a beat. "I do know you're pregnant, and I think it's wonderful! And this job with me would be perfect for a woman with a newborn. I expect most of your work will be with Luisa at our home, so of course you are welcome to bring the baby along. We can be very flexible, especially at first, since Luisa will be spending a great deal of time at the college participating in a study Dr. Bidwell is working on right now. It should be exciting."

"It sounds fascinating, I really do think so, but, Anna--"

Oh, Samantha, I'm not finished," she sped along. "You will be an employee of Anna Victoria's Pies, and as such you will be entitled to all the benefits that comes along with that. We offer a very comprehensive health insurance plan of course, also dental and vision coverage. We have twelve paid holidays a year, in addition to four weeks of paid vacation time, and ten days of sick leave per year—which you may accumulate if you wish. Our benefits package is better than almost any private company, and certainly rivals any public entity." She took a breath, but held up her hand as if signaling for more time. "Now, Samantha, I can see you want to say no, and I can understand that. This offer is new, and very sudden. It would mean a significant change in your position, your place of residence, well, in just about everything. All I ask is that you don't reject me out of hand. Think about it."

"Anna," Samantha pleaded, " I could say that I'll think about it, but I'd just be stringing you along. I really don't want to do that."

"You may change your mind, Samantha--"

Samantha shrugged. "I don't think so--"

"No, wait," Anna interjected. "I haven't told you everything yet." She paused. "There is something more."

Samantha said nothing, just raised her eyebrows.

"Yes, okay." Anna licked her lips. "What I haven't told you yet is that I'm not sure when this will happen. Maybe it won't happen at all—though I can't wrap my mind around that yet." She looked over at Samantha, suddenly very vulnerable-looking.

"Did something happen to make you change your mind?" Samantha asked slowly.

"Yes," Anna said firmly. "Something very surprising—and disturbing. Here I had everything planned out. I have my people back east looking for a house for Luisa and me! Looking at schools! But just this morning, well, I asked Luisa what she wanted for breakfast, and instead of saying waffles or cereal, she started in telling me the story of how she was born down in Peru. The story of her mother and father." She shook her head. "There is no way she could know this story."

"Was she accurate?"

"Yes, she had details that were shocking."

"And you know it's all true?"

"It's consistent with the story I was told," Anna nodded. "Of course, the sisters at the orphanage didn't know everything. But still--" Her voice drifted off.

Samantha said nothing; she sat with her hands on her lap, waiting for Anna to go on.

"There's only one way she could have typed that story," Anna said finally.

Samantha leaned forward, truly curious. "What is it?"

Anna sighed. "I must have been guiding her hand. There's no other explanation. How could there be?"

Samantha nodded, initially surprised that this would be Anna's assumption. But of course, to Anna this was only logical. "Could Luisa, you know, have overheard you talking to someone?"

Anna shook her head. "I haven't even thought of this story for years!" she exclaimed. "They told me in the orphanage when I came to pick her up. When I got back home to California, I told my own mother the story. Yes, Luisa was in the room—she was in my arms!—but she was only 14 months old. She couldn't have overheard and remembered this story when she was only a little over a year old. That's not possible. And then, you know what? I haven't told this story to anyone else—ever."

"Maybe your mother told someone recently, when Luisa was in ear shot?"

"No, Samantha," Anna said sadly. "My mother died when Luisa was three years old. Even if she did say something in front of Luisa, I don't think Luisa would have remembered it."

"So you're convinced you were guiding her hand?" Samantha said.

"I guess I'm hoping you'll have another explanation, but I can't think of any." She smiled sadly. "I have so cherished these past few months, getting to know my daughter! She seemed so genuine. Do you think I made the whole thing up?"

"Anna," Samantha reminded her, "we have had some verification. Nothing startling, but small events. She told me about the weekend you took her to Monterey to see the aquarium. She told you about the times we baked cookies and made pancakes."

"You bake nearly every Friday. That's not a big surprise. What I can't understand is why I would guide her hand?"

"*If* you guided her hand," Samantha cautioned. "Don't be so hasty."

"Well, it certainly seems strange," she continued. "Why—when we were running around in the morning trying to get ready to get to school and to work—why would I decide to guide her hand and tell such a story? It doesn't make sense! But I don't know what else to believe!" She looked at Samantha, seemingly very tired. "You know, it's a very sad story. . ."

Samantha reached forward and touched the other woman's arm. "Wait, Anna," she said. "Luisa told me a story too."

"What?"

"She told me the story of her birth. Let me tell you what she said—I mean, there's no way I could have known the story and guided her hand, is there? Let me tell you before you tell me the 'correct' version."

Anna nodded cautiously. "Okay."

"Okay—it was a month or so ago," Samantha started. "She said her mother was very young, 11 years old. She said her mother's older brother wanted to sell her into prostitution, that he could have gotten a very good price for a young virgin. But a friend of her birth mother—a boy not much older—I think she said he was 13—he made love to her—to protect her, so she couldn't be sold as a virgin. Of course what the young people didn't count on was that the girl would be disowned, thrown on to the streets. And the brother chased off the young father, threatening to kill him. The sisters found the young birth mother begging on the streets as she was entering her ninth month. But it was too late. She bled to death in childbirth, but Luisa was saved."

"Oh my God, Samantha; I can't believe that's possible! But you didn't know the story. You couldn't have guided her hand, could you? Somehow she had to have known! I can't fathom. . ."

Samantha looked over at Anna, and she felt a little scared, as if a secret were about to be revealed, and she wasn't sure what the reaction might be. "Samantha," she asked with a leading lilt in her voice, "you don't think—do you think it could be possible that Luisa, uh, that she could have some kind of psychic ability?"

Samantha nodded slowly. "I don't think we can discount anything, Anna."

Anna narrowed her eyes. "Do you believe this kind of thing is possible? I mean have you always believed?"

Samantha felt a jolt of adrenaline hit her throat. She took a deep breath. "I'm a very spiritual person, Anna. I guess I believe that God works in mysterious ways."

Anna looked solemn. "I'm not that way; I've always been very pragmatic, seeing is believing, you know what I mean? But this—this rocks my boat, Samantha! I don't know what to think."

"Your daughter is very special, Anna," Samantha said softly. "I guess right now that's all you need to know."

Anna grinned. "I guess so! And I guess the move east is back on." She grasped Samantha's hand. "Please consider it!"

"Anna, I--"

Anna held her finger to her lips. "Not another word. Save it for another day. I know you're bound to give it some thought."

"Well, Anna, let me say this: I'll bet it's pretty darn cold in upstate New York this time of year. I'd think twice about moving to Syracuse in January."

"Oh, Samantha, I guess I forgot to say—the professor is no longer in Syracuse; he's at Yale. We'll be moving to New Haven. In Connecticut."

Samantha's breath caught in her throat. Charlie's mother lived in New Haven. This was the city he was talking about moving back to. She bit her lip. Was this the sign she'd been asking Craig to give her?

"New Haven," Anna repeated optimistically, obviously noting Samantha's reaction. "You have some connection there, Samantha? Maybe I can get you interested now?"

"I, uh, well--" she stammered.

"Just think about it," Anna insisted again.

Samantha suddenly felt she was in a dark quiet place where she could hear her own heart beating. She knew what she needed to do, what she needed to say. She couldn't go rushing across the country with the intent of blackmailing a man into loving her, just because she had his baby in tow. That was not how she wanted to live her life. She shook her head.

"New Haven, Syracuse, it really doesn't matter, Anna: the answer will be the same."

Anna shrugged and stood up. "If that's your final decision I respect it, Samantha. But we'll have lots of time to talk before Luisa and I leave. If you don't mind sharing, I'd like to know more about these spiritual views of yours."

"I look forward to it," Samantha said genuinely. "I'm going to miss Luisa."

"She'll miss you too." Then Anna surprised her with a hug. "I'll be in touch."

CHAPTER TWENTY-TWO

Samantha drove slowly home in the twilight, smiling at Christmas lights twinkling on her neighbors' houses. Reindeers and nativity scenes, glitter and holly wreaths were everywhere. "I'm happy," she thought. "I'm actually happy."

One more week of school before winter break. She promised herself she would tell a few co-workers about her pregnancy before vacation. She knew others often made big announcements at staff meetings or sent out emails, but she knew that word would spread quickly if she told a few select people. It would be easiest that way.

She pulled up to her house, then floored the brakes, stunned. A half dozen sturdy yellow-billed magpies stood pecking on her green lawn. "They're back!" she said aloud. "West Nile Virus didn't kill them! They're back."

She pulled into her driveway and the birds took off. "You won't get away that easily," she called after them, laughing at her own eccentricity.

Angelcat greeted her inside then followed her to the bedroom. She pulled on her favorite faded jeans but she couldn't get them zipped anymore. She was tempted to scream in frustration, but what was the point? Time for a trip to the maternity department, she decided. Can't hide it anymore.

She succumbed to an old pair of yoga pants that stretched

easily but hid nothing. A T-shirt and cardigan completed her frumpy ensemble. Stealing a glance at herself in the mirror, she knew there was no denying her condition.

In the kitchen she fed the cat then foraged through cupboards and fridge for mushrooms, spinach and garlic to add to an omelet. Or would it be easier to eat a can of chicken noodle soup? As she stood on the cold Mexican tile in her stocking feet, torn between fatigue and internal admonishments to eat healthy for baby's sake, the phone rang. "Hello?"

Charlie's cheerful voice greeted her. "Hey, Sam—how are you, girl?"

Samantha boosted herself onto a stool at the kitchen counter. She was finally relaxed, ready to share her news. "Hey, Charlie. How are things in Connecticut?"

"Cold!" he said. "I guess California has spoiled me, Ms Omm. I don't know that I want to go back and live through an entire winter of snow again."

She took a deep breath, almost afraid to ask. "How's your mom?"

"Well, Sam, she's still hanging on. She's one tough cookie, you know. Paralyzed on one side, but they still get her up for physical therapy nearly every day, and she's not doing too badly with the speech therapy. She's amazing." He paused. "Anyway, she's in a nursing home now and my sister and I are talking about selling her house—but stuff like that is sometimes too hard to talk about. We decided to give ourselves a break, so I've come back to California for Christmas."

Samantha sat up straighter, daring to hope. "Are you back in town?"

"Yep, I'm home."

"Gee, Charlie," Samantha said slowly. "I think this is the first time I've ever heard you call Sacramento home."

"I know," he said, and Samantha could detect no irony in his tone. "Well—you know what?" he continued. "I missed you, Sam. I couldn't stop thinking about you. I know you just got out of a marriage, and maybe the timing isn't right, but I'd really like us to give it another go. You don't have to make any promises yet, but--" He sighed. "I want to be with you, Sam. Can we talk?"

Samantha stood up quickly, nearly leaping in joy. "Yes!" she said. "I'd like that."

"Can I come over?"

"Right now? Sure! How long will it take you to get here?"

He laughed. "It'll take about thirty seconds. I'm parked outside your front door."

"Really?" she squealed, finally unafraid to show her feelings. "Come on in."

She hung up the phone and rushed to the door. She peeked out a small high window, watching him get out of his yellow car. She patted her swelling abdomen, knowing that the moment she opened the door, she need say nothing more. She held her breath as he came up the path. His head was framed with white Christmas lights from the house across the street. His face was radiant, his smile child-like and eager. As he stepped onto her porch she could see his entire body was suffused in turquoise light.

ACKNOWLEDGMENTS

I was blessed with wonderfully supportive parents, Andy and Bernice Schoellkopf. Although they've both passed on, I want to start by thanking them as I suspect they are still within earshot. Thanks also to the rest of my family, particularly my brother, Andrew Schoellkopf, my cousin, Joanne Brust, and my surrogate sister, Diane Aubery Alexis.

I am very grateful to be welcomed into a vibrant community of talented writers including Carol Schultz, Roxann Phillips, Matt Dittrich, Deborah Kelch, Feliz Moreno, and our leader, the incomparable John Crandall. Your support throughout this endeavor has meant the world to me. (And a shout out to John's wife Denise, who welcomes us into their home every week.) Thanks also to my dear sister writers Leslie Rose, June Gillam, and Carmel Moir, and my amazing readers, Sue MacDonald and Tara Stiles.

I would be remiss if I did not mention the elusive yet inventive HC, who has done a fantastic job serving as muse.

And finally to my dear friend Craig, who relocated his consciousness way too soon for my liking, I send out this post card: *Having a wonderful weekend. Wish you were here.*

ABOUT THE AUTHOR

Nancy Schoellkopf has been telling stories and writing poems for many lifetimes. It goes without saying she's needed a second income, so this time around she happily taught amazing children in special education classes in two urban school districts in Sacramento, California. A full time writer now, she enjoys lavishing attention on her cat, her garden and her intriguing circle of family and friends. Contact her at her website: www.nancyschoellkopf.com

www.ingramcontent.com/pod-product-compliance
Lightning Source LLC
Chambersburg PA
CBHW020617180626
46810CB00007B/2818